Confederate Paydirt

Gentleman Jim Murphy was content to play high stakes poker until he heard about the gold; Billy wanted to avoid his former confederate, tough ex-Union Sergeant Joshua O'Donnell; Seraphim Angel McCall wanted all she could get; and nobody trusted anybody. Not the best of starts when the four banded together to form an unlikely partnership to search for the long lost Confederate bullion, especially since they were up against the redoubtable Zachariah Holmes and his murderous band of comancheros.

The trail began in Madison and led into the trackless wastes of the hostile, sun blasted desert, where the intrigue redoubled with treacherous plots and counter plots flying as fast as the bullets.

The gold may have been there, but would anybody live to retrieve it?

Confederate Paydirt

Robert Anderson

A Black Horse Western

ROBERT HALE · LONDON

© Robert Anderson 2010
First published in Great Britain 2010

ISBN 978-0-7090-8867-7

Robert Hale Limited
Clerkenwell House
Clerkenwell Green
London EC1R 0HT

www.halebooks.com

Typeset by
Derek Doyle & Associates, Shaw Heath
Printed and bound in Great Britain by
CPI Antony Rowe, Chippenham and Eastbourne

CHAPTER ONE

WINTER QUARTERS

Winter held the country fast in its grip, and even way down south in New Orleans the rain-fat clouds hung in a cold and miserable cloak over the town. Not that the rain outside ever troubled Gentleman Jim Murphy, or disturbed his sure concentration on the game. He played cards to earn his living, and that meant poker. More fastidious souls than he might have considered the superficial gloss of the Mississippi Palace an unsuitable background to their trade, but Jim knew to the cent how much his partners at the tables could be taken for and where all their weaknesses lay. The Palace might have allowed the riff-raff in to play, but his table was reserved for only the richest of clients, and he dropped a regular supply of gold coins into the manager's pockets to ensure that that happy state continued to apply.

The manager prided himself on his ability to pick out the best of his clients, and Jim was one of his favourites. Gentleman Jim, they called him, a tall, well-built man, who earned his sobriquet with a relaxed air of distinction and his habit of playing in a neat, stylish suit, complete with waistcoat, crisp white linen shirt and bootstrap tie. His habit of tying a gun low on his thigh, holstered in well-worn, but recently oiled leather was, of course, regrettable, but for that he was not entirely to be blamed when one considered the black-hearted crew that made up the major part of the Palace's patronage. He never started any trouble, always maintained his polite and friendly front and, best of all, he was generous with his money.

Play had been quiet on the day until Gilt Bartram turned up. He and Jim were old adversaries, and although Jim seldom made any profit from playing the older man, he liked to match his skill against someone as good with the cards as himself. The table was made up by a fat drummer sporting a lavish wad of cash, and known to them simply as Walt, and a weasel-faced, slim Jim drifter, called Billy Harkness. Jim knew a piece of Billy's history, but he'd never played a hand with the man, though they'd shared a drink at the bar on more than one occasion.

The session resolved itself at an early stage. Gilt played with his usual quiet skill and was an early winner, but without any spectacular pots coming his way he soon began to see his profits dwindling away. Jim's long streak of luck finally deserted him, and only a stony-faced resolve kept his losses to a minimum while he waited for the run of the cards to turn his way. The drummer played big and won big, taking all the luck and by far the best of the bigger pots, leaving Billy to bear the brunt of the losses. He'd built up a stake on the outlying tables, stealing the biggest pots more by sleight of hand than any skill, and that lack of innate ability had shown him up against more experienced exponents of the game.

'Damned if the luck don't seem to be going my way at all,' he grumbled, adroitly shuffling the pack before the next deal. 'How come you get all the breaks, Walt?' Billy stared directly at the drummer.

'Don't play if you can't take a loss.' Walt's cavalier return, which owed as much to the drink he'd taken as his dislike of the other's whining voice, gave no joy to Billy, who flushed angrily.

'I can cut you down to size any day,' he boasted, and began to deal, skimming the cards across the table with fleet-fingered ease.

The next few hands seemed to echo his

sentiments. For a while the luck seemed to run Billy's way, until an ill-judged reliance on a lowly two pair saw him begin to lose big time again. This time the reversal of fortune left him almost at a standstill, as the thin stack of coins at his elbow testified.

It was make-or-break time, and he gambled everything on the turn of a card, recklessly betting the balance of his cash against the drummer's stake once Gilt and Jim had folded. The fleeting echo of a smile dawned over Walt's florid face when Billy showed a nap hand of kings with a whoop of delight and reached out to haul in the pot.

'Not so fast, little man.' Walt staged his own show, judging to the second just how long to drag out the moment for the greatest discomfiture of his opponent, before he tossed down his own cards. It was a winning straight flush, and he gurgled wickedly in triumph.

For a moment Billy sat immobile, barely able to believe the evidence of his own eyes. He'd been certain his four kings would win, betting his all on the outcome, and the other's unexpected twist of fortune left him pale with anger.

'You're a damned trickster,' he told his tormentor emotionally.

'Nobody labels me a cheat and gets away with it,' the drummer snapped at his beaten foe. 'I don't take such filthy insults from no one, most especially a dirty little weasel like you.' He flung back his chair and hauled a pistol out of his belt with tolerable dexterity.

'Put the gun up.' Nobody had seen Jim move, but the gun was in his hand and trained relentlessly on Walt's heart.

'You heard me first time,' he continued with cold-eyed clarity when the drummer looked likely to dispute the command. 'Do yourself a favour and settle this without gunplay.'

'Damn the pair of you for bad losers.' Walt shoved the pistol back into his belt with ill-concealed fury. 'I'll take my winnings and leave.' He began to rake in the pot.

'Not just yet, friend.' Jim indicated his own losses and the remaining few cents left at Billy's elbow. 'If Billy's right about your play, you've taken a liberty too many around this table.' He allowed the gun barrel to drop a tad, but didn't return the weapon to its holster. 'Not much we can do about what went before, but he'll be glad to replay this round.'

With the drummer on the back foot, Billy didn't look as though he'd be glad to do any such thing, but he couldn't refuse outright, not when Jim still had a gun in his hand. And in the end it wasn't necessary.

'Not likely. He can keep the pot.' The drummer was gathering up his cash and even the offer of a replay wasn't going to change his mind. Jim might have looked like the gentleman he was named for, but he most certainly wasn't acting like one. Walt had seen the spark in his eyes, and knew he was in the presence of a man who was prepared to kill if it came to it.

Billy, more relieved by the conclusion than he cared to admit, swept his winnings off the board and decided to leave it at that. The stakes might have been lower at the outlying tables, but winning was easier, and he too had noted the ease with which Jim handled his gun. A little manual dexterity had always been a feature of Billy's game, but he wasn't going to attempt sleight of hand under the nose of a notorious sharp shooter.

'Was that wise?' Gilt Bartram asked the gambler when they were alone.

'Management don't like to raise a ruckus in here,' Jim answered easily. 'It might bring the law down on them.' He grinned engagingly. 'There's other things going on around this saloon, besides a fight over a hand of cards, that the marshal might interest himself in. This is my base for the winter months, and I wouldn't want to risk it for the sake of a drunken drummer,' he stared after Billy, 'or a down at heels loser.'

'Was Walt cheating?'

'Maybe. Maybe not.' Jim spread his hands in a dismissive gesture. 'If he wasn't, he had a streak of luck as wide as the river in flood, but I was watching close, and I didn't catch hide nor hair of it. He let Billy take that final pot mighty quick for an honest man, though.'

'Luck has a funny way of choosing partners, Jim. You didn't single him out for that reason.'

'He was all set to shoot Billy when he'd been going out of his way to provoke him all night.' Jim sighed. 'I shouldn't have let the old fool play at our table in the first place.'

'Could you stop him?'

'No one plays at this table without my permission. Billy's tried before, and I only let him in this time to make up the numbers. Guess I hoped he was a better player than I'd tagged him for.'

'You didn't have to step in to save his miserable hide. That drummer was drunk enough to turn his gun on you.'

'Even Billy doesn't deserve to die for the sake of one ill-considered remark.' Jim shrugged off any attempt to present him as a hero.

'He doesn't look the sort to put himself out for anyone, even an old friend.' Gilt appeared to be watching Billy step up to the bar, but his gaze was carefully assessing the gambler.

'I dare say he wouldn't.' Gentleman Jim Murphy found himself in complete agreement with the other's sentiments. 'Not that I'm an old friend either.

11

More of an acquaintance. I've only known him for a couple of months, and even then I've done nothing more than share a drink or two with him of an evening, both here and on the river.'

'Damned if I don't like you, Jim.' Gilt clapped him on the shoulder. 'Think on it before you take up the cause of a man like Billy, though. He's mean and evil, through and through.'

'He's not the best of company when he's in his cups,' Jim responded in the manner of a man who knew. 'He's idle and feckless, mean too, if you like, but evil's taking it a tad too far.'

'Your life, Jim,' Gilt agreed. 'Will you be staying on at the Mississippi Palace for a while?'

'I'm a fixture here until next spring, then I'll move back on to the Queen for the season. The grand saloon in a river boat of that quality's too rich a meat for me to leave alone.'

'I'll see you around then. No point in continuing to play today.'

CHAPTER TWO

BILLY HARKNESS

'Let me buy you a drink, Jim.' Billy Harkness's voice was already slurred in the fumes of the potent spirit by the time Jim reached the bar.

'Whiskey.' He nodded to the barman. There was no need to tell him to use the bottle of best Kentucky rye that he kept hidden beneath the bar. Jim was good for a generous tip, and well the barkeep knew it.

'Thanks for facing down that goddamned cheat.' Billy was inclined to be maudlin and Jim cursed under his breath. 'He'd have taken all my money and shot me down too, if you hadn't interfered.' Billy staggered and held on to his companion with an owl-eyed hoot of laughter. 'Sorry,' he muttered. 'Reckon all this liquor is getting too much for me.'

'You ought to retire to your bed,' advised Jim, carefully judging the state of the man's inebriation.

Billy wasn't as old as he looked, but then he wasn't young either, perhaps in his late forties. His wizened, weather-beaten face added years to his age, and his lean-shanked, spare frame, shorter than Jim's by a full head, didn't do anything to deny that calculation. He'd acquired a certain measure of cunning over the years, a guile that served to keep him alive, and ingratiating himself with Gentleman Jim Murphy was one of his principal aims.

The gambler recognized this, though he was never quite sure of the other's reasons for doing so. Billy was good enough company when sober, but inclined to become tiresome when in his cups.

'I ain't got enough cash to bed one of the girls and get out of town.' Billy began to count through his small stash of money. 'A man needs money to travel. Reckon that drummer should have stumped up more than he did. He was taking us for fools all night.' He belched loudly and sagged against the bar. 'You ought to have beaten it out of him.' He stared balefully at his companion as though Jim himself had diddled him out of his due. 'Lend me a dollar or two?' he requested and belched again. 'Just enough to buy me a bottle and a girl?'

'Not likely.' Jim was disgusted by the other's

drunken antics and turned him down flat. 'In your state you won't stand up long enough to drink your way through another bottle, let alone take a girl upstairs. Anyhow, where're you going to go in the middle of winter?'

'It ain't healthy around here no more.' Billy spoke hangdog fashion, but his wary eyes were flickering watchfully around the saloon, and for a moment Jim could swear the alcohol induced haze had disappeared from them. 'I saw him this morning.'

'Saw who?'

'Sergeant O'Donnel.' Jim suddenly realized the man was truly frightened. 'Bloody Sergeant O'Donnel. He's the very devil himself, and he's got it in for me ever since . . .' Billy's voice trailed off abruptly and he peered around suspiciously as though his nemesis might suddenly materialize at the bar.

'Spend what money you've got on drink and girls,' advised the gambler shortly, wondering what Billy had been about to reveal. 'There's no need for you to run from anyone. New Orleans is big enough to hide in.'

'You think I'm flat broke, don't you? A worn-out saddle tramp with no more than a dime or two to his name.' Billy's voice rang out louder than he intended and in an abrupt reaction he suddenly dropped it to a more conspiratorial tone. 'You're

15

right,' he admitted, 'but I could be an important man. Honest, I could be rich. Have all the drink and girls I want.' He looked around suspiciously, as though to spy out who might have heard him boast, then carried on in a barely heard whisper. 'I know where there's a pile of gold, just waiting for someone lucky enough to go pick it up. It's lying out in the hills, only just out of reach.'

'I've heard you talk about that gold before, Billy,' Jim told him wearily, 'and it's always when you're fall-down drunk. If you know so much about the secret, how come you're not rich already?'

'It ain't so easy.' Billy began to whine and Jim sighed. He was too goddamned soft.

'Time for bed,' he told Billy. 'I've got a room upstairs. You can sleep it off on the floor.' He caught hold of the man and began to steer him towards the stairs, but they'd barely taken the first two steps before the older man's legs began to buckle. Jim effortlessly hauled him over his shoulder and strode on up the stairs.

It was several minutes before Jim returned to the bar. Billy was snoring loudly, laid out on the floor with one rolled-up blanket under his head and another spread out over his body to keep out the cold.

'Whiskey,' he signalled the barman.

'Would you like to buy me one too?'

16

Jim stared at the girl who'd joined him at the bar and considered the request. He nodded. 'Make that two, Joe.'

She cosied even closer. 'Thank you.'

Jim looked her over curiously. He'd seen her before. Not just this evening, but other nights too. Given her ample charms, he could scarcely have missed her. A striking redhead, attractive and confident, she was taller than most of the women he knew. Still young too, no more than her early twenties, if that, and dressed in the latest fashion. Her gown was deliberately cut close and low, displaying her trim figure with more ostentation than the average young miss about town would see fit, but it was at least more modest than the attire normally favoured by a girl from the saloon.

Why had she approached him tonight? She wasn't one of the saloon's own girls; he knew them all by sight. Nor was she an outsider on the prowl. If that were so, she wouldn't have been allowed to ply her trade at the Mississippi Palace; the management took a cut out of everyone's purse. Come to think of it, though he'd seen her passing the time of day with several men, he'd never seen her leave with one.

'Jim Murphy,' he offered.

'Gentleman Jim Murphy, or so they tell me.' The barkeep set a glass in front of her and she raised it towards him. 'You don't get many of those around the Mississippi Palace.'

'Do I know you?' Jim suspected a set-up.

'Seraphim Angel McCall,' she told him, daintily holding out the back of her hand for him to kiss. 'You can call me Sera.'

'You play cards,' he spoke the words as though accusing her, while he swiftly ruffled through his memories.

Yes, Sera played at the tables, he decided, but not often. Not the richer end of the market where he operated either; she sought out her marks on the main floor of the saloon. Easy pickings for a woman owning sufficient skill with the cards, and who was prepared to use her feminine wiles to reel in the victims. Did she want to play with him?

'I have played,' she admitted, 'but I'd never measure up to your standards.' She leaned forward confidentially. 'I watched you play tonight. With Billy Harkness and the others.'

'You did?' For the life of him, he couldn't work out where Sera was going. She wasn't coming on to him, though he had the most ungentlemanly feeling she would if it became necessary.

'You saved his life.'

'Billy?' Jim began to ponder whether, despite the difference in their ages, she had a *tendre* for the man. He contrasted her youthful form with that of Billy Harkness and decided he must be mistaken.

'You're awful fast on the draw. That drummer didn't stand a chance. I hope Billy was duly grateful, or are you two friends from way back?'

She didn't know Billy after all, Jim decided. Billy had no friends; come to that, neither did he.

'We've shared a drink or two,' he admitted cautiously, suddenly aware of how he was being pumped.

'Has he spun you the story of his gold?'

'Why on earth should he do that?' Jim automatically returned the non-committal answer. He was sorely tempted to laugh out loud that the fanciful tale should have been believed so widely, but instead he kept a straight face and went on to explain. 'I met Billy on a riverboat, took a drink or two with him, but he doesn't know me well enough to confide in me. Not secrets, at any rate.'

'I overheard him tell you just now,' she confessed, 'and I'd lay long odds he's spoken about the gold before. He was drunk too. A man like Billy says a lot of things when he's drunk. You can make some sense out of his words, then all of a sudden it's just maudlin rambling.'

'There's no sense at all in his blabbering,' Jim argued forcefully. 'He's just drunk enough to boast out loud. If he had a stash of gold waiting to collect, we wouldn't see him for dust.'

'He's told me about the gold too,' the girl replied.

'Told me where to find it. Close enough, anyhow.'

Jim could well imagine it. Sera would have laced Billy with drink and promises until she got the complete story out of him.

'We could pool our knowledge,' she continued, moving in closer and dropping her voice to a husky whisper. 'If you want to take me upstairs . . .' She allowed the unfinished offer to ride in the air, only snuggling up to him to show the promise was real.

'Billy's sleeping in my room. We can't go there.' Jim had a sudden, unexpected suspicion that Sera wasn't all she seemed. The meaning in her offer was unmistakable, but so too was the bloom in her cheeks. Despite her nonchalant attempt at seduction, the woman wasn't quite the calculating harpy she portrayed, and the gambler was left wondering whether she'd deliver on her promises.

'I have a room too,' she quavered, putting an end to his suspicions. 'We could go talk there, if you like.'

'What about Billy? Seems like this here gold's his secret.' Jim began to perceive how serious Sera was, and found himself tempted to see just how far she'd go for the sake of the precious metal.

'Perhaps we could cut him in for a share.'

'Unless this stash of gold only exists within his head.'

'It doesn't. It's real, all right. He has a map, he told me so, even let me catch a glimpse of it. Unfortunately it shows no more than a part of the complete picture. One of his companions holds the remainder.'

'Companions?' Jim did laugh this time. 'What companions? I've never known Billy take up with anyone regular.'

'I thought you might be one of them. You're the only man I've ever seen take any interest in him. Do you have a map?'

'I neither have a map, nor believe a word about this cache of gold. If there ever was gold lying about waiting to be collected, then someone somewhere has already collected it.' Jim shook his head in sheer frustration. The girl evidently believed in Billy's fairy tales and, despite her reservations, was even prepared to sleep with him for a share in the imaginary treasure trove.

'It's way out in the wilderness,' she told him shortly, stung by his disbelief. 'Guarded by the Apache.'

'In that case it can stay out in the wilderness. I'd sooner keep my hair on my head than undertake some fool expedition into Indian country.'

'I can tell you more, Mr Murphy, honest I can. Billy might have been drunk when he showed me the map, but not too drunk to convince me. All we need to do is find the other map.'

'Sounds just a little too easy.' Jim snorted derisively. 'But I suggest you get off to bed before I take advantage of your original offer.'

'What about. . . ?'

'Good night, Miss McCall. It's been a long day, and I'm too tired to be playing games at my age.'

CHAPTER THREE

CONFEDERATE GOLD

Next morning Billy was badly hung over and inclined to question his saviour's motives for intervening between him and the drummer.

'I was drunk last night,' he admitted. 'Did I thank you properly for saving my life?'

'You did, or as good as.' Jim Murphy watched his overnight guest warily. There was an air of uncertainty about him.

'I wasn't too polite, was I?' Billy hunched his shoulders petulantly. 'I'm not when I'm drunk, but I am grateful to you.' Then in a much more suspicious voice. 'What else did I tell you?'

'A pack of damned lies,' returned Jim lightly,

though he was beginning to wonder about the authenticity of the tale. Billy Harkness was making more of the story than a mere tissue of lies would deserve. *Unless he's about to touch me for a loan again,* he decided, *and that's much more likely.*

'Have I told you them before?'

'You've hinted you're not as poor as you look.' Jim's noncommittal answer seemed to satisfy the man.

'I talk too much after a bottle or two. Don't pay it any mind.' Billy stared straight at Jim's face as though to discover just how much of the story he believed. 'Fact is, I'm broke,' he told the gambler candidly. 'I saw Josh O'Donnel in town yesterday and realized I had to get out before he discovered I was here too. That pot you saved for me is all I have in the world.'

'What does he want with you?'

'Nothing.' Billy's answer was guarded and gave none of his secrets away. 'Leastways, I hope not. He's got a murderous temper when he's crossed.'

'Shouldn't think he'll pay you any mind.' Jim didn't really care, so long as Billy didn't remain in his room. One night spent with a man who snored so ferociously was enough to cut up his peace of mind.

'He'll want to take care of me.' There was a hint of truthfulness in the little man's face that caught on Jim's imagination.

'Why?' For once in his life he found he had an

interest in Billy's answer.

The other hesitated a moment, then lowered his voice to a whisper. 'It's to do with the gold.'

Jim groaned when that old chestnut took shape, but strangely enough he began to feel drawn into the story. His companion had evidently decided it was time to look for an ally. Would he open up?

'Before the war we were. . . .'

'Before the war?' Jim interrupted his guest, barely able to believe his ears. 'The war came to an end nearly twenty years since. If you're expecting a handout for some cock-and-bull story, then you can think again.'

'Before the war,' Billy continued with unexpected imperturbability. Now he'd begun his confession, he intended to finish. 'I was a soldier in the army, and in particular, part of a cavalry force on detachment at a lonely outpost way out west. We were barracked at a small fort, or more truthfully, a wooden stockade, built up years before, with a garrison about forty strong. I don't know why we were posted out in that god-forsaken, sweltering sweat-box of a wilderness, no doubt the officers did, but they never told us troopers, not even the sergeant. Guess it was to hunt Indians, but one day when we were out on patrol, a score or more of us, led by a lieutenant, we came across a Confederate wagon train.

'They'd already seceded, but we weren't yet

officially at war with the South back in those days, so the lieutenant rode on in with a couple of the men. The sergeant,' Billy stared hard at Jim as though daring him to contradict, 'Sergeant O'Donnel, that is, led me and a couple of the others further up the hillside to establish a watch. Told us he didn't trust them damned Southerners as far as he could throw them, and he was right about that at least. We'd barely started our climb before we heard the shooting. Couldn't see nothing from our position to the lee of the hill, but it was obvious the Confederates had opened up on the lieutenant and his party and as soon as we breasted the rise we could see the battle developing. Most of our men were down, dead or wounded, and the rest of the patrol had stormed in to their aid.

'It was one hell of a fire-fight and we were just about to join in from our vantage point when the Apaches arrived. They were all painted up ready for war, and O'Donnel reckoned afterwards they'd probably been tracking the wagons for days. Just bad luck our fellows happened on those damned Southerners at the same time as they attacked.

'Bad luck it was, too – those damned savages just seemed to erupt out the ground in all directions. Our patrol and most of the Confederate escort were caught out in the open and wiped out immediately, while the remainder pulled their wagons into a circle and tried to fight back. Josh, Sergeant O'Donnel, ordered us down. There weren't nothing we could do to help them, and well he knew it. We just lay there, hidden from their sight on top of the hill, shivering with fear and waiting for the end to approach. It didn't take long neither, a couple of hours, more or less. There were only five wagons, and with most of their escort already slaughtered, the teamsters were heavily outnumbered.

'Their lives were on the line and they knew it well enough to put up one hell of a fight, but the Apache eventually overran them, just before sundown. Luckily for us, it was getting dark by the time those savages got around to plundering our horses, otherwise they'd have spotted our sign for sure. Anyhow, eventually they fired up the wagons and pushed off. We could hear them whooping into the night with the flames lighting up their red skins and highlighting the paint like a scene from hell. It was a long night, as you can imagine, but in the morning there was no trace of the savages, just the acrid stink of smoke and death.

'We didn't really know what to do, but eventually trooped down to see if anyone was still alive. Foolish idea, and we should have known better – all we did was scare ourselves witless. Nobody could have survived the Indian's onslaught, not when those damned savages had mutilated each and every

27

corpse. A couple had their throats cut too, presumably because they'd still been alive when the Apache braves reached them. Left us in a desperate plight too, the horses were all gone and the wagons were a mess. Those that hadn't been burnt completely through were charred wrecks.

'That's when we found the gold. We were miles from anywhere civilized, facing a forced march in the sweltering heat. We needed supplies, especially water, and began to plunder the least damaged of the wagons. Luck was on our side, we hit pay dirt first wagon we searched. The gold had been hidden under a false floor, but the fire had charred through the wood and exposed the shiny metal. We were all rich, riches beyond our dreams, but then we were all dead men too. Or would be if we couldn't find water.

'Josh took to organizing us then. We'd degenerated into a disorganized rabble from the scale of the disaster, but the prize ahead heartened us, especially him. We found a couple of water butts the savages had overturned, but with enough liquid still left in them to refill our canteens, and a charred joint of jerked beef. Ruined by the flames and smoke, but desperate times make desperate men and we filled our bellies in spite of it.

'The fort was several days distant on foot, and there was precious little chance of anyone forming a relief column. We'd have to leave the gold, but Josh had plans for that too. "It's ours," he told us. "We'll hide it and bring back a wagon to collect it later." Damned if I knew just how heavy the gold was going to be. Josh had scouted out the narrow gorge of a box canyon, little more than a slit in the line of the cliffs, several hundred yards distant, and we carried the ingots a few at a time. Must have been a couple of hundred of them, and it damned nearly killed us all. By the time we'd completed the task our water was running low again, but before we left Josh set us at work to start a landslide. There were tons of loose rock and shale higher up the slopes and we soon started a slide big enough to cover the gold and hide the canyon opening. Anyone spotting that jumble of rock wouldn't even realize the gorge had ever existed, let alone guess at the treasure buried underneath.

'The march back to the fort was a nightmare. We were all of us cavalrymen, and neither we nor our boots were used to walking. God alone knows how we made it, maybe the thought of how we'd spend our riches helped. Nevertheless, make it we did, but not all of us. We started the march with five men, and finished it with four. Josh told us later that Pat died in his arms, but I reckon he murdered him, though I didn't suspicion it then, not until much later. Not that any of us would've complained if he had confessed to it. Pat had been the only one to hold out

29

on keeping the gold for ourselves. He told us we should inform the army of our find, thought they'd reward us. Huh, some hope of that!

'None of us would have made it at all if the major hadn't thought to send out scouts when the patrol didn't return on time. They found us strung out along the trail, in a state of collapse, dying from exhaustion and lack of water. We soon perked up back at the stockade, though, and made our plans to desert that very night and return to collect the gold with a wagon. Josh told us them pesky Indians would soon be gone, they were only out there to trail the Confederates. No one, not even them poor savages, lived all their lives out in those conditions.

'No such luck, as I guess you've already worked out.' Billy's face crumpled into a woebegone mask. 'Before we could act on our plans, the major told us we were pulling out right away. New orders had arrived along with a strong cavalry detachment from further west. The war against the Southern states had begun and we were caught up in it with no chance to skip out of line. Deserters were no longer flogged, they were shot on the spot, and not even Josh was willing to run that risk. Besides, the Southern states had no more than a ragtag army. We'd be back out West before the year was out.

'The map was Josh's suggestion too. He reckoned we'd soon find ourselves lost in the arid, rocky landscape, where one landmark looked too much like another. Tom Bigold was the only one of us as could draw and we commissioned him to do the job. He drew it from memory in two parts; one of them showed step-by-step instructions on how to locate the Confederate wagons and the other identified the exact position of our canyon. He reckoned it'd be safer to divide the risks, we'd have to trust one another, but in reality he was drawing up a death warrant for any one of us who didn't have a map. We drew straws to see who took which of the charts. Sergeant O'Donnel was in charge, and it was no surprise when he took first choice, the bigger of the maps. Then it was my turn to get lucky, a location map with instructions clear enough to get me to the site.

'In the event, the reality of war didn't match our hopes of a quick return. The fighting was fierce, and we spent our time fleeing from battle after bloody battle before the North began to get on top. By this time, we formed a part of Grant's victorious army, but even though Lee was under the cosh, the battles just seemed to get bloodier. Petersburg was one of the worst. Johnny Wesson got his there, and that's when I began to suspect O'Donnel was guilty of systematic murder. I always reckoned Johnny was the bravest of us all, but he took a bullet in the back, and that was a battle we didn't need to flee from. The war seemed to go on for ever, but their retreat down the banks of the Appomattox spelt the beginning of the end for those damned rebels. Then Tom was shot down by a sniper – he'd been on sentry duty at a forward camp. We were in a dangerous position and it could have been for real, but Sergeant Josh O'Donnel was out hunting for our supper that evening.' Billy let the aura of suspicion lie like a gossamer-thin veil over his recital.

'Next day I took a bullet too. For real this time. Josh came to visit me while I was with the medics. I was raving in a fever and like to die, but even so, I saw him going through my kit. I was too fly for him, though. I'd hidden the map too well for anyone to find it.

'It was years before he found me again. I'd been sent north to recuperate and then posted to another regiment after the end of the war. Took me two more years to work my passage out of the army and travel west again. There's a settlement out there now, a place they call Madison, a mile or two east of the old fort. Started off as a trading post where the wagon trains heading west could rest and pick up water, but it's grown since I first went there – ranch houses, a bank, a couple of saloons.' Billy shrugged eloquently. 'Josh was there too, threatened to kill me if I let anyone else get a sight of my map. Would have stolen it too, I'm sure, but he daren't risk slitting my throat when he didn't know where it was hid.

'The old fort was still garrisoned, but the Indians had their war parties out, and we barely escaped with our own hair when we made our first expedition. We needed help, enough armed men to protect our backs, and that cost money. We teamed up with a couple of drifters and took the bank, nearly got clean away with the cash too, until the sheriff took a hand. Our new friends were killed when the posse ambushed us, I caught a bunch of lead in my belly and Josh and I both drew fifteen years' hard labour.'

Billy looked sick and clutched his stomach as though reliving the moment. 'It ain't no fun being dragged around by a sadistic sheriff when you're gut-shot,' he offered. 'I hung on to my map though, and was lucky enough to draw a different prison from O'Donnel, else he'd have had it off me while I was still too weak to prevent him. I finally got out last year, a free man at last. I took a trip out to Madison straight away, but things have got worse.'

'Are the Apache still there?'

'No, they've all been pushed further out west, or forced on to the reservations. The soldiers have gone too. The old stockade's deserted, but there's still a problem to be solved. A bunch of Comancheros are living out there now, led by a man called Holmes.'

'Zachariah Holmes?'

'That's right. How d'you know about him?' Billy

was instantly on the defensive. Jim didn't look like a Comanchero, but there was no telling what a man might do when the gold beckoned towards his soul.

'Most folks who've travelled out west know of his reputation.' Jim reflected on what he knew of the bloody misdeeds attributed to the vicious outlaw. From all he'd heard, Holmes was worse than the Apache; a venomous snake and definitely a man to avoid.

'He's got a gang of no-good rattlers running with him,' confirmed Billy. 'They raid the nearest towns and ranch houses at will, and retreat back into the wilderness before the law can get to them. God knows where they've found a place fit to live in that god-awful wasteland, but the townsfolk in Madison swear they've made a regular settlement out there. They kill anyone they find exploring the desert too, just in case they're lawmen out to make a reputation.'

'So you still need an army?'

'Yeah, no lawman's going to risk his life clearing out that nest of vipers.' Billy sniffed. 'All that gold just waiting to be picked up, and I ain't got hold of enough money to do it.'

'What about Holmes himself? He might split the gold with you.'

'I've got too much respect for my life to seek him out. Zachariah Holmes ain't a man to share anything, let alone a parcel of gold.' Billy made the statement into an accusation.

'I reckon you're right there,' confirmed Jim. 'That sounds just like the Holmes I heard tell of.'

'I started gambling then. Hoped to make enough money to fund my own party, but I never seem to get there. I've won a pot or two, big ones sometimes, but I always hit a losing streak sooner or later.'

'What about Sergeant O'Donnel?'

'Josh got out a week or two later, meaner than ever, and the word is out he's looking for me.'

'Looking for the map, you mean?'

'Yeah, but I won't let him see hide nor hair of it.' Billy's lips curled into a sneer. 'He'll kill me for sure once he gets his hands on that chart.'

'What do you want from me?' Jim felt certain Billy hadn't entrusted him with the secret of his gold for no good reason. He wasn't drunk, and neither had he held back on the gory details. He was sure it was due neither to friendship nor trust. Billy didn't trust anyone, and that made for mighty bad friendship.

'You've got money and connections. You could fund an expedition. A parcel of gunmen to protect us. We could both become rich men.'

'What about O'Donnel's map?'

'We can do without it. Once we've located the site, we can scout around. The Confederate wagons will still be mouldering out there – the air's far too dry for them to rot. It happened a long time ago, but it can't take us long to identify the canyon once we've found those.'

'I don't think so,' decided the gambler, albeit regretfully. He was beginning to believe in the story, but there were too many outstanding issues that Billy had glossed over in mooting an expedition. 'I'll lend you the money to escape Sergeant O'Donnel, but no more than that. I'll be shipping out on the Queen come the spring. You can pay me back then.'

CHAPTER FOUR

THE MISSISSIPPI QUEEN

Gentleman Jim Murphy leaned reflectively on the teak rails that surmounted the gingerbread cast-iron railings around the deck of the Mississippi Queen. Spring had arrived early and while he stared into the colours of the misty sunset, he began to think again of Billy Harkness and his peculiar story of lost Confederate gold. Far below, the broad waters of the Mississippi River rippled, winding like a snake through the densely forested back country, shrouded by a gentle fog that grew out of the lowering sun. The sound of crickets chirping and the abundance of

Spanish moss added to the atmosphere of a chilly Southern evening.

The boat was one of the largest and grandest on the river, and a particular favourite for the gambler. Its decks towered high above the quays, a floating palace of gingerbread fretwork and fluted stacks, spewing thick, blackened smoke into the rapidly darkening sky. He strolled down the deck aft, the twin split stern wheels turning lazily in his path, as he ducked through an entrance and headed for the stairs. The interior was all hardwood panelling, teak handrails, ornate trim and polished brass fittings. The grand staircase was crowned by a many-branched crystal chandelier, lighting a *trompe l'oeil* ceiling depicting cherubs cavorting in the clouds, but he barely noticed its magnificence.

He reached the foot of the staircase and entered the lavish extravagances of the grand saloon, a place to see and in which to be seen during the day, but transformed every evening into a ballroom which also hosted the nightly entertainment. It looked more like an opera house than a ship's saloon, complete with a proscenium stage at one end and a row of private box seats on the mezzanine level. During the day a black combo, principally brass and drums, alternated their play between New Orleans style marches and the increasingly popular syncopated, creole music they called ragtime. The adjoining Louisiana lounge hosted a bar and the best of the gaming-tables, those at the far end, on a slightly raised platform, reserved for the highest of rollers such as himself. The heavy brocaded curtains were furled, and hadn't yet been drawn against the night, their decorative swags hanging heavily from the ornately carved lintels. The stained-glass windows were styled on the latest fashions from Paris, France, but Jim had no eyes for such frippery. He'd caught a glimpse of Billy Harkness, slipping cautiously up a back stairway.

It was the work of a moment to slip through the fashionably dressed throng taking their ease before dinner, and race up the narrow stairway after the man. At the next level he was greeted by a short length of corridor, empty; he cursed under his breath. The barest click from a closing door decided him. Half a dozen strides and he flung it open. The echo of retreating feet drew him forward, the space was dark and uncomfortably warm, and the thud of heavy machinery oppressively close. The engine room couldn't be far off, and neither could Billy.

'Jim.' The man himself suddenly appeared from behind a set of rough metal shelves. 'Is it really you?'

'Damn it, Billy, you know it is. Where the hell are we?'

'The crew use this space as a dry store, the engine room's just below. Passengers are strictly prohibited.'

'Then what are you doing here?'

'Hiding,' Billy admitted frankly. 'I spotted Josh O'Donnel taking a drink down in the lounge. Damned if I knew he was even on the boat.'

'O'Donnel? Is he on board too?' Jim Murphy knew the ex-sergeant was the man he needed to meet if his nebulous plans for the gold were to be brought to fruition. 'Describe him to me.'

'Big fellow, ugly as sin.' Even Billy realized this was unlikely to satisfy the gambler's curiosity and he continued to make his description more carefully. 'About your height, maybe a tad higher, but much broader, chest like a barrel and strong as an ox. His face is as thickset as his body, with a nose looks like it was broken years ago. He's tried to disguise himself with the bushiest beard I ever did see, but I'd know him anywhere. Black, but streaked with thin skeins of grey, same colour as his head. Damned if I know how he does it. He's years older than me, but he's still covered in hair.'

Jim paid the complaint no mind, since he knew Billy was over-conscious of his own thinning locks. 'What's he wearing?'

'Dark serge suit and matching vest with a white necktie.' Billy stared at Jim suspiciously. 'You're not going to tell him I'm here?'

'I am.' Then he softened the threat with a word of comfort. 'I'll guarantee your safety if you're willing to

40

take me on as a partner. Otherwise there's no point in me seeking out O'Donnel.'

'Partner?' Billy looked seriously put out until Jim explained himself.

'I've some sort of a plan to put to you. I can't explain it now, not until O'Donnel is on board too. It's his secret as much as yours. Would you be willing to cut me in on the deal if he was? Equal shares for us all. I'd put up the money to fund the expedition and take it out of the proceeds as expenses.'

Billy nodded. 'Sure thing, Jim, but we don't need O'Donnel along. I swear I could find the gold without his share of the chart.'

'It'd be much easier for us all if he consented to the deal,' asserted the gambler. 'I'd rather not remain in Zachariah Holmes's backyard for any longer than necessary, poking about without a map to guide us, and neither do I want to spend my time looking over my shoulder, wondering if your precious sergeant's about to shoot me in the back. We'll need more labour than the two of us anyhow. You've already told me how heavy gold is, and the more hands we have to collect it, the better, especially if they're strong as an ox.'

'Not Josh O'Donnel, Jim. He's sheer poison.'

The gambler could see how frightened Billy was, but he remained adamant. The expedition wouldn't set forth without the big ex-sergeant's inclusion.

'Stay here, and I'll fetch you when it's necessary,' he conceded at last. 'If O'Donnel won't accept me as a partner, there's no need for me to tell him about you.'

Josh O'Donnel proved easier to track down than Jim had expected. Once the gambler had stepped into the bustling lounge there was only one man who could have matched the description Billy had given: an inch or two over six foot tall, a chest the size of a water butt, and sporting thick, curly, jet-black hair and full beard. The man was ordering at the bar, towering over the other customers.

'What's your poison, mister?'

O'Donnel turned to survey the neatly dressed gambler warily. The muscles in his thick, bull-like neck ran in taut, bulging cords under the neckline of his vest and he shook his head emphatically.

'I'd like to buy you a drink,' Jim persisted.

'I don't know you.' The other's eyes were dark with suspicion, his lids hooded. Josh O'Donnel wasn't a man who accepted drinks from strangers. Long experience had taught him they were rarely free.

'I don't know you either, Mr O'Donnel,' Jim told him, thrusting out a hand, 'but we have at least one mutual acquaintance. If I get the drinks perhaps we can talk about him.'

'Billy Harkness!' The big man caught on quickly

and his words were spelt out clearly and with bitterness. 'He's a blabber mouth, and so I've told him before.' Jim had expected an Irish brogue from the name, but Josh O'Donnel was pure bred Yankee. 'Is he on board?'

'I am,' Jim told him shortly, 'and I've got a proposition to put to you.'

The big man nodded. 'Whiskey,' he told the gambler, 'but I don't want to discuss my business in public.'

'Fair enough,' conceded Jim readily, signalling a barman to get the drink. He was surprised how easy the big ex-sergeant had been to convince. According to Billy, he'd been more likely to twist his head off than speak to him. 'I've a stateroom up above the observation deck.' He handed the other a key. 'You've ample time to finish your drink and join me there. I've got my partner to collect.'

O'Donnel's hand snaked out and caught hold of Jim's shoulder in a firm grip. The hand was the size of a ham and despite the other's age, Jim could sense the strength in his fingers, just as he could distinguish the rippling depth of muscle in the big man's arm, even through the thick, serge suiting.

'No partners. If you've got a proposition, put it to me yourself. I don't need anyone else involved, and I'll break you into little pieces if you try to double-cross me.'

This was more like the man Billy had described, and Jim grinned engagingly. 'An old friend,' he promised and brushed the other's hand off his shoulder. 'Don't go imagining I'm like Billy,' he warned. 'The boot will be on the other foot if you try to cross me once we're declared partners. I'll shoot you down like a mangy dog.'

The big man only grunted, but Jim knew he'd got his attention.

Sergeant O'Donnel had evidently been in the stateroom for some time when Jim and Billy arrived. He was happily ensconced in one of the overstuffed armchairs that formed a part of the furniture, having helped himself to a shot from Jim's own store of whiskey.

'Very impressive,' he conceded, holding up his glass in salute.

'Yeah.' Billy evidently thought so too, his eyes roaming about the room. It was bigger than any cabin he'd seen before, but kept snug, spick and span. He took in the elegant, patterned wall coverings, thick, warm, inviting patchwork quilt over the oversized solid wooden bed and the solid wooden shuttered windows. 'Cost you a pretty dollar or two,' he ventured.

'Are you in this with him?' O'Donnel broke the ice first, his eyes boring glacially into Billy's slender frame.

'I suppose so,' confirmed Billy, beginning to back off from the other's threatening attitude.

Jim could see there was no love lost between the pair and quickly intervened. 'Mr Harkness has agreed to hear my proposition, just as you have.'

'Billy's a damned cheat and liar, Mr—' O'Donnel stumbled over his words. 'Who the devil are you, anyway? How d'you come to know my business? And why should I trust you?'

'I'm known as Gentleman Jim Murphy. My business is gambling. Ask anyone who knows the river, I'm recognized on most every boat that's still afloat and a few that aren't.'

'I suppose Billy told you about the gold.' O'Donnel's voice was harsh. 'He never could hold his liquor. Neither can he deliver any gold without my share of the map.' He laughed. 'We hate each other like a blazing fire, but neither of us can find the gold without the other.'

'He's agreed to an equal partnership if he likes the look of my proposition,' Jim put in mildly.

'Has he now? That's easy to do when it's not his share to give.' For a big man, O'Donnel moved fast. Before Billy could dodge him, his throat was caught fast in one giant hand.

Jim Murphy's own reactions were just as fast. His pistol rested against a throbbing nerve in the big man's head.

'Leave him be, mister,' he commanded, ignoring Billy's frightened wail. He deliberately cocked the weapon, the click sounding loud against the silence of the suddenly still room. Ex-Sergeant Joshua O'Donnel slowly let go of his quarry and faced the gambler, his eyes still hot with anger.

'If you ever pull a gun on me again,' he warned, 'then you'd better be prepared to fire, because if you don't I'll rip your heart out.' He sat down and glared at Billy balefully.

Billy sat down too, tottering as far as the free armchair and collapsing into it, gently stroking the livid marks where the big man's fingers had sunk into his scrawny neck.

'Next time I'll shoot,' Jim promised. An element of truth shone through the devil-may-care look on his face, and not even the angry sergeant could mistake his meaning. Jim Murphy wasn't a man to be easily dismissed, and neither was he a man accustomed to issuing empty threats.

'What's your proposition?' O'Donnel had composed himself, though he still gave Billy a dark look.

'That I fund an expedition to go out and collect the gold. The three of us only, equal shares after expenses are taken into account.'

'Why should I agree to those terms? Billy either? We have the maps. Without those, you'll get nowhere.'

'Agreed,' affirmed Jim with a trace of a smile on his face, 'but then neither can you. I assume you don't have the money to fund a successful expedition, and neither do you have a viable plan.'

'Do you have a viable plan?' O'Donnel stared at the gambler with more interest, his face alive to the possibilities. He knew that money to finance an expedition was the least of their worries.

'I know how the Comancheros operate.' Jim was aware, even as he spoke the words, of how apocryphal they were. He'd run with a wild bunch when he was young, but they'd never sunk to the depths of outright villainy. Zachariah Holmes would be a killer, like all his gang. He'd still be smiling while he pulled the trigger on his own mother.

'Their sort don't have friends.' Josh O'Donnel's voice rang out bleakly. 'If knowing how they operate is all your plan's got to offer, then you can leave me out of it. I've had my fill of crazy schemes.'

'Have you met Holmes yourself?' The big man's answer had stirred a chord in the gambler.

'I met his men,' O'Donnel replied grimly, 'and I barely escaped with my life.'

'You're a lucky man,' Jim told him. 'From all I've heard, not many men survive when Zachariah Holmes wants them dead.'

'I got together with a couple of old teamsters ,' the big man explained. 'They told me how they'd run into a parcel of burned-out wagons several years before. That was before Zachariah Holmes blew in, of course, but they reckoned they could take me right back to the spot, Holmes or no Holmes. My map could take up the story from there.'

'And cheat me out of my share.' Billy put in his bitter dime's worth.

'You weren't anywhere to be seen, or I'd have taken you along,' O'Donnel claimed, then struck back. 'Pity you weren't – I wouldn't have to listen to your whining voice if your bones were lying out there, meat for the vultures.' He sighed gustily and continued his story. 'We barely got out of town limits before them ornery rattlers hit us. Someone must have been spying on us. Someone who knew exactly what was going on.' He paused. 'I wondered if it was Billy at first,' and shot a darkling look at the smaller man. 'Anyhow they shot down my partners, but saved me for questioning by Holmes himself.'

'Then they know about the gold?'

'They must suspect its existence at the very least,' Josh O'Donnel replied wearily, 'only Holmes never got the chance to interrogate me. It takes a whole heap of rope to keep a man my size tied down and I skipped camp before he arrived.'

Jim stared at the evidence of the banded muscle in the man's arms and believed him. Strong as an ox,

Billy had said, and Billy, for once in his life, wasn't exaggerating.

'Did they find your map?' he asked.

'The map's as safe as it always was,' confirmed the sergeant. 'I memorized it immediately after the war. Every line and mark, every word of it, is safely stored in my head, rehearsed and re-rehearsed every day while I was confined to jail. The map itself is buried in a deposit box, and no one but me will ever learn of its hiding place.' He turned his attention back on the gambler. 'You still haven't spelt out your plans,' he told him.

'Zachariah Holmes himself is the key,' Jim told his companions calmly. 'He won't trust us an inch further than he can throw us, but toting enough whiskey will provide the ticket to get us in. We'll drive a couple of wagons loaded up with booze, and set up a travelling saloon for him and his men.'

'How will you know where his camp is?'

'They'll lead us in once they've taken the bait, but not to his camp. We'll insist in setting up our quarters closer to the gold.'

'Holmes won't believe a word of such a crazy cover story. No one's going to take such a chance to sell a few bottles of whiskey.' O'Donnel dismissed the plan out of hand.

'We'll play our ace in the hole once we've arrived. The wagons will be specially adapted with a false

49

floor. We'll be running guns out to them too.'

'He won't believe that tale either.' Josh O'Donnel told them bluntly. 'More likely to take the guns and shoot us out of hand.'

'It may serve long enough to give us time to locate the gold,' argued the gambler. 'If we don't take some risks, we'll never make our fortunes.'

'We can hide it under the false floor on the return trip.' Billy Harkness had suddenly turned enthusiastic.

'No.' Jim Murphy silenced the man abruptly. 'If Holmes suspects us, and he will, he'll search under there for sure. We'll have to modify the wagons further. There'll be some hard work involved, but if we carve out a groove in the underpinnings it'll give us space to store the gold. We'll have to melt it down ingot by ingot and pour it in, but once it's in place and given a coat of axle grease, no one's likely to discover it.'

'It's a pretty rough trail to follow.' O'Donnel seemed to have accepted the plan at face value. 'Won't do for the wagons to break up, going in or going out.'

'We can add extra strengthening to the underside once we've got space for the gold prepared.' Murphy added a stark warning. 'We may not be able to recover every cent of it this trip, and I, for one, won't be going back in.'

'Long as we get enough for the three of us,' O'Donnel grunted. 'What happens if Holmes don't fall for any of this?'

'We're all dead men,' replied the gambler, 'probably die painful too. That's why you're going to shave off that beard tonight and have your hair cut back. Holmes may not have seen you, but from what you say, some of his men have. A man as big as you is bound to draw their attention and all that hair makes it easy to recognize you. A clean-shaven face and short hair might just serve to save our bacon.'

Josh O'Donnel stroked his beard reflectively and nodded. 'Fair enough.' He pointed towards Billy Harkness. 'Do we really need him?'

'What do you—' Billy's aggrieved outburst was silenced by Jim's answer.

'He has hold of the location map. Could you find the burned-out wagons without it?'

'I doubt it, but I'm willing to make the attempt.' O'Donnel glared at his former companion. 'He just ain't to be trusted, especially where there's hard liquor or women around.'

'I'll keep an eye on him,' promised Jim faithfully. 'Are you in?'

Josh O'Donnel nodded, then held out one huge paw to shake the gambler's hand. 'Long as he's got the map.'

'He has.' Jim Murphy stared at Billy, who was

beginning to squirm uncomfortably in his chair. 'You do have the map, Billy?' he asked suspiciously.

'Fact is . . .' Billy looked sheepish and stumbled over his words. 'Well now,' he began again. 'It's like this.'

'Where is it, Billy?' Jim was aware that O'Donnel's notoriously short fuse was about to blow.

'It's somewhere on the boat, I reckon.'

'Tell us where.' Josh O'Donnel had risen to his feet and stood menacingly over the smaller man.

'All right, so I lost it.'

'Lost it?' Jim Murphy and Josh O'Donnel ejaculated in unison. For once their thoughts were as one.

'One of the women took me down to her cabin last night. I've met her before and she's real keen on me, but I'd had too much to drink and she must have rolled me. Then someone woke me up and stuck a gun in my face. Turns out it weren't her cabin after all. She'd picked this guy's pocket and stolen his key. Took me a couple of hours to talk my way out of that one.'

'If she's still on the boat, then all we have to do is find her.' Josh O'Donnel simplified the question for them.

'Seraphim Angel McCall.' Jim Murphy breathed her name out loud.

'Yeah, that's right,' Billy returned. 'Do you know her?'

Jim Murphy didn't even attempt an answer. 'Has she come on to you too?' he asked the big ex-sergeant.

'Met up with her in Natchez a month or two back,' Josh admitted. 'Sort of name a man remembers. Sort of dame he remembers too.'

'I'll bet she stood real close,' Jim offered.

'Sure did.' Josh grinned at the memory. 'The bar was crowded, but she didn't have to sidle up that near. She's got a real sweet body, but we did no more than pass the time of day.'

'Lucky you don't carry the map around with you.' Jim let the comment ride while he silently slipped across to the cabin door. 'She's come on to all of us, one time or another,' he continued conversationally. 'Real handy for her to have such nimble fingers.'

He flung open the door, grasped hold of the woman listening outside and threw her in.

CHAPTER FIVE

SERA ANGEL MCCALL

'What are you doing?' Sera was magnificent in her red-faced rage, playing her part as the indignant innocent to perfection. 'Is no woman safe on this ship? Leave me be, sir.'

'Damn you for a slut.' Billy, once he'd got over his surprise, leapt up to accuse her. 'Where's that map you stole from me?' he roared, thrusting his face close up against her own.

Sera slapped him hard across his cheek, the pale outline of her handprint stark against his flushing anger. 'I'm no thief, you damned liar,' she screamed and plunged backwards towards the door, only to find Jim Murphy lounging at his ease against its bulk.

54

'Let me out immediately,' she commanded, still attempting to play the grande dame.

'Strip her,' suggested Josh O'Donnel calmly. The girl was trapped and he, for one, had no intention of letting her escape. 'If she's got the map hidden on her person, we'll find it.'

'Yeah.' This was one suggestion from the ex-sergeant that Billy was prepared to follow. He began to taunt her. 'Take your clothes off, darling, or we'll do it for you.' He laughed harshly. 'She won't get the chance to escape me this time. Nor anyone else as cares to try her.'

Sera looked scared for the first time, and backed off from her tormentor, but her ruse had been spotted by the gambler and he stepped up close behind. The tiny gun appeared in her hand from nowhere, but Jim, having already realized her intention, moved just as swiftly. One long arm snaked around her body and plucked the gun from her hands before she could do any more than threaten her molesters.

'She sure can act good, but she's deadly as a poisonous snake,' he admitted when he threw the weapon to Josh O'Donnel, who caught it with a dexterity that belied his bulk.

'Twice as treacherous too,' agreed Billy and threw a roundhouse slap at the girl, heavy enough to knock her down if it had connected.

Jim caught it on his forearm and warned his angry partner. 'Go sit down again, Billy. We won't get anywhere by knocking her about.'

'Too right you won't, mister.' Sera turned angrily on the gambler. 'I'm not so stupid as to carry the map around with me, even if I have got it, which I'm not admitting.' She glared unabashed at her captors.

'What then?' O'Donnel kept his temper with admirable resolve. 'I still say we ought to strip her. We need that map to locate the gold. If it isn't on her right now, and I'm not convinced of that, we can try more drastic steps. I dare say she doesn't want that pretty little face of hers marked.'

'If you've been listening outside, you must know the map's useless to you without O'Donnel's input.' Jim tried the common-sense approach on the girl. 'It shows no more than the location of a couple of burned-out wagons, and you wouldn't get that far before Holmes's Comancheros hit you.'

'What makes you think you would?' Sera hit back.

'Just how much of our plans did you hear?'

'Enough to know how valuable that map is. If you're lucky, Holmes might allow you into his territory to set up a travelling saloon and trade guns with him, but you'll never get out again if he spots you trailing up and down after a bunch of burned-out wagons. He's no fool, and your only chance of bluffing him is to settle down directly over the gold.'

'What do you suggest?' Jim turned the problem over to her. 'We could search you garment by garment like Josh says. We might find the map that way.'

'Have fun trying, too.' Billy was still up for that suggestion.

'If you did, what's to stop me running off to Holmes and blowing your cover? He might be willing to offer me a share of the gold.' Sera laced her speech with all the venom of a woman delivering a bombshell.

'Not if we knock you on the head and push you overboard.' Josh O'Donnel spoke quietly, but there was no doubting the menace behind his words. He stared hard at the woman, who fell back before his angry assertion.

'Cut me in for a share,' she told them desperately, suddenly realizing that at least one of them was prepared to go as far as killing her. 'Sure, I've got the map, but so what. You won't find it without my help. Take me on and I can tend bar as well as any of you, and sing too if you want.'

'Sing? That might be useful. Are you any good?'

'I've got by singing in saloons in my time,' she asserted. 'I'll never be signed up by the opera, but I can hold a tune, and you'll need extra muscle to load up all that gold.'

'Damned if I'll give up another share,' Josh

O'Donnel exploded. 'Take a woman along and it won't be long before every cowboy between here and the west coast knows our plans.'

'I can hold my secrets,' Sera snapped back. 'Hold my drink too, which is more than some people can.' She stared deliberately at the shrinking figure of Billy Harkness.

'Four equal shares,' Jim decided. If he waited for the rest of them to agree to a plan, they'd still be on the boat come Thanksgiving.

'Damned if I will.' O'Donnel hunched his bull-like shoulders and prepared to defy them.

'You will,' Jim informed him confidently. 'Either we all go, or I'll pull out and you can make your own arrangements. Equal shares ensure no one has any reason to double-cross the others.'

Josh O'Donnel grunted in a gesture of non-committal, then just as suddenly changed his mind and stuck out his hand towards the woman. 'Reckon Jim's right,' he admitted, nodding his head, 'but I'd just as soon not have a woman riding along with us.'

For a moment Sera looked as though she'd ignore his overt move towards friendship.

'Look lady, once I shake on a deal, I don't back out.' He aimed a derisive glance towards Billy. 'Can't swear it's like that with everyone in this room.' He offered his hand once again, and this time Sera took it.

Billy Harkness repeated the gesture with less than good grace. 'Where's my map?' he asked her.

'Good and safe,' she assured him quietly, slipping one dainty hand into her bodice to draw it out in the manner of a conjuror pulling a rabbit out of his hat.

'Damn it, I knew we should have searched her,' howled Billy. 'We could have saved ourselves a quarter share.'

'Only at the cost of silencing her,' Jim reminded him. 'We'd have been strung up if we'd been caught disposing of her body, and this river boat's far too crowded to be sure of escaping justice.'

'She can pay for her passage, can't she?' Billy licked his lips and advanced on her shrinking form.

'Back off.' She spat directly in his face, then adroitly caught the little derringer that Josh tossed back to her.

Billy dropped back. Sera looked as though she possessed the gumption to use the little gun. 'We got to offer them outlaws a woman,' he whined. 'Holmes will expect it. They all will.'

'I don't whore for any man.' Sera flicked up the gun and aimed it directly at Billy's midriff.

'He's got a point,' Josh O'Donnel mused. 'Likely they will expect whores. If Sera doesn't want the job herself, she could act as madam.'

'Sure, I've done that before now,' the girl agreed. 'Long as I don't have to lie with anyone myself.'

'No whores.' Jim appointed himself as arbiter on the question.

'They'd keep Holmes's men busy,' remarked Josh.

'Keep them in camp longer than we'd like, too. We can't move gold while they're out and about. Nor while there's anyone else watching us, either. If you want to bring a whore along then you'd better be prepared to offer her a share, or she'll surely betray us all.'

CHAPTER SIX

SETTING OUT

The township at Madison was voted in as their kick-off point. Jim Murphy and Sera Angel McCall provided the advance party, ostensibly freshly married and seeking to establish a business in agricultural machinery maintenance, for which they'd purchased an old blacksmith's premises. The convenience of owning spacious single-storey living-quarters overlooking the wide pasture at the rear of the open-fronted barn that housed the forge was too good to be missed.

Josh O'Donnel, Jim's surrogate father for the benefit of the more curious of their neighbours, rolled in a few days later, piloting a massive prairie wagon hauled by six heavy, solid-boned work horses. Its capacious well carried the bulk of the heavy equipment and ironwork they'd need to convert their wagons. No point in purchasing such items in Madison when it would only raise local suspicions above the usual inquisitive murmuring to be expected at the arrival of any new inhabitant. Billy Harkness, their supposed uncle on her side, followed on in a second wagon. He was hauling a load of surreptitiously acquired liquor and modern repeating rifles, though these again were commodities that remained a well-kept secret from the local citizenry.

Their cover story of being agricultural engineers was soon made all the more credible by their enterprising attempts to dismantle the wagons prior to cutting out the grooves in their underpinnings to take the gold. Josh O'Donnel had enough experience at the blacksmith's trade to teach the basics to Jim, and the pair of them toiled at their self-imposed task for virtually all of two long weeks, before they eventually and successfully refitted the wagons with additional strengthening bars. Billy had displayed an unexpected flair for working with wood, and made his contribution by constructing false floors for each of the wagons, while Sera, when she wasn't assisting one or other of the labourers, spent her time feeding and watering both them and their stock.

They largely kept themselves to themselves so far as the town was concerned, too exhausted to do much more than fall into their cots at night. Hard work, but the magnetic lure of the waiting gold drove them on, and not even Billy Harkness, the most feckless among them, seemed to have any intention of shirking his responsibilities.

Their departure was as mysterious as their arrival. They set off in the early hours of the morning while it was still dark outside, the hoofs of their horses bound up with cloth, and anything that moved on the wagons freshly greased to make their exodus as silent as possible. The scintillating flare of a desert sunrise hit them when they passed the old fort, its deserted stockade outlined starkly against the cascading colours of the open sky, silently watching over the beginning of their journey into the sun-seared wilderness.

Josh O'Donnel led the way, as massive as he was silent on the prow of his prairie wagon. In his wake rolled a smaller wagon, captained by a jubilant Billy Harkness with an equally ebullient Sera McCall at his side. Jim Murphy scouted ahead on a saddle horse, seeking out the easiest path across the rocky landscape while still avoiding the deep-filled traps of soft sand which could so easily bog down their heavy vehicles. He was no longer dressed as the gentleman, no longer the foppish gambler, but a whipcord-hard, trail-toughened boss, sporting the trademark gear of his profession. A cotton twill shirt overlaid with a leather waistcoat, tough denim trousers, leather chaps, tooled and spurred boots and a wide-brimmed sombrero to shade his face from the merciless sun. His scarred leather belt together with his pistol in its well-oiled holster remained the same, but this deadly armament had been augmented by the long, slim outline of a rifle carried in a workmanlike scabbard slung from his saddle.

Their first encampment lay in the lee of a steep sided cliff, its friable rock crumbling under its daily torture of sun and wind. The day had seemed relatively easy after the backbreaking toil of their preparation work in Madison, and they sat around the campfire discussing the journey and the dangers inherent in attempting to fool the Holmes gang.

'Do you reckon Holmes robbed that train?' Billy asked the question that had exercised all their minds to one extent or another. News of a violent strike against the railroad had reached town only the day before. The courageous engineer had spotted the gang and organized a bloody defence that led to an indiscriminate slaughter of passengers and crew.

'It's just the sort of bloodshed he'd enjoy,' Josh joined in dismally. It was an opinion the town marshal had agreed with, though he was careful to point out that it was way out of his jurisdiction. Just as well, since he'd have found it well-nigh impossible to find enough men willing to set themselves up against Holmes to provide himself with a deputy, let alone form a posse.

'Any massacre within a hundred miles of here will be attributed to Holmes,' Jim told them easily. 'It doesn't make a whole lot of difference to us whether he did it or not, but we'll start by setting guards tonight.'

'There's no chance of Holmes running across us here,' objected Billy. 'If he hit the railway, he'll be counting up his profits back at camp. Besides, it'll be two full days before we hit his territory.'

'This is all his territory,' Jim returned shortly. 'Some of his Comancheros could be watching us right now. It's best we get ourselves organized right away. We'll have to set watch sometime.'

Josh O'Donnel grunted, a sound Jim took to mean approval. The big man wasn't very talkative, but he had a way of making himself understood.

'That's settled then. Billy, you take first watch. Wake Sera in two hours sharp. I'll take the next watch, then Josh. I want an early start tomorrow, so we'll turn in right away.'

'OK.' Billy gave an ostentatious yawn, and settled back against a convenient boulder while the others began to roll out their blankets.

'If you nod off during your watch, Billy,' Josh

O'Donnel warned his partner, 'I'll peel the hide right off your miserable frame, even if I have to use a blunt knife to do so.' In another man it might have been construed as a joke. From the big ex-sergeant it sounded like the sinister warning he meant it to be.

Jim Murphy didn't stay awake long enough to check on Billy's wakefulness, but slept until Sera gently awoke him in the early hours, traditionally one of the most difficult shifts.

'There's a convenient place to keep watch up above,' she whispered. 'Come on, I'll show you.'

Sera led the way up a narrow fault in the cliffs behind to disclose a natural hollow that overlooked their camp and gave a wide field of view across the wilderness beyond.

'I spotted it last night,' she told him.

'Well done.' Jim stared when Sera hunkered down beside him. 'You'd better get some sleep,' he suggested.

'I don't feel like it yet,' she admitted. 'The sky's too big for me out here. I prefer to live close by other people.'

'It's big, all right,' Jim agreed. He stared at the girl; he knew all too little about her. They'd lived on top of each other in Madison, but somehow never had the chance to speak of anything other than their immediate work. 'Seraphim Angel McCall,' he mused. 'That's quite a mouthful.'

66

'My mother's choice.' Sera went quiet and Jim thought for a moment that that was all he'd get out of her, but it appeared she was in the mood for confession.

'She was Irish born, a devout Catholic from the far western peninsula. Her parents sold her into service with the local nobility – best a girl could hope for during the famine. I guess she must have been a beauty in those days because the son of the house took up with her, preying on her innocence, and convincing her she was the love of his life. Turned out it only amounted to a dose of lust and he dropped her when he found she was carrying his child. She was thrown into the streets without a reference, of course, but somehow managed to take ship to America, where she brought me up.

'I suppose I ought to thank her, but all I can remember from my childhood was the sheer, grinding poverty and the strictures of her religion. She was no longer pretty and beat me for the slightest deviation from the ways of the Lord, then made me pray for forgiveness. And if she didn't beat me, then Father O'Connor would – for wilfulness, for vanity, for the sheer bloody hell of it.' Sera's voice held an edge of suppressed anger. 'I ran off as soon as I was old enough to know what I was doing. I was pretty enough to live on my wits, swiftly discovering how easy it was to twist a man around my finger. And if I couldn't fool them any other way, I'd trade my body for the soft life their money bought.'

She sighed. 'I'm not a good woman, Jim. Nor ever likely to be.'

The velvet silence of night settled about them again until she asked him the same question. 'Gentleman Jim Murphy is quite a mouthful too.'

'I wasn't born Gentleman Jim.' He smiled. 'I was brought up on a small ranch by my father. I don't remember much about my mother. She died when I was still too young to mourn her. But unlike you, I had a happy childhood, working and playing on the land, until Pa died too. He'd gone away to war, leaving me in charge of the farm, until he fell at the Bull Run. Guess I'd have stayed on working the ranch if a couple of old soldiers hadn't happened along. They reckoned I was far too young for such a responsibility and took the ranch away from me, but if they'd reckoned on me leaving peaceable, then they were wrong.'

He thought back on the bad times, then decided to be as frank as Sera had been.

'I was brought up holding a gun and determined to make them damned soldiers pay. Shot it out with the pair of them and left them for dead. That gave me the ranch back, or so I thought until the sheriff came calling. He knew me too well to draw a bead on me, only warned me to make a run for it before a posse came after me. I took his advice and drifted out West, where I met a wild bunch of youngsters, homeless like myself. We were friends for a while, living off the land and our wits, shooting our way out of trouble whenever a ready tongue couldn't talk us out it.

'One of them had a violent streak that disturbed me sometimes. Ambition too. He wanted to lead his own gang, and talked us into making an attempt on a bank. We'd never travelled that road before, but he'd heard how one of the local banks was pulling in the deposits and decided to cash in.'

Jim Murphy waited in silence for a moment or two before he went on. 'Someone else got there first,' he told her sadly. 'There was a posse waiting and they shot them down like dogs. I didn't know them, of course, but it could have been me being dragged down the street towards the undertakers, could have been my blood sucked up by the thirsty dust.'

He laughed. 'Our leader still wanted to go ahead and rob the bank. Told me the timing was ideal – nobody would expect a second attempt so soon after the first. I told him no, and he shot me down.

'Doc put me back together. I was lucky, I'd gone down and been left for dead, but his slug missed anything vital. A couple of months later, I rode out good as new and took a legitimate job, surveying for the railroad. Pa had taught me enough about theodolites and the maths that went with them to persuade them to take me on. God knows where he learned it. Started to play cards on the job too, and found I was naturally good. Good enough to start gambling for a living – precariously enough until I learned my trade, then I graduated to the riverboats. There's always a mark prepared to drop big money in the grand saloon.'

CHAPTER SEVEN

COMANCHEROS

Time passed quickly and a couple of days later Jim Murphy awakened to the smell of coffee being brewed over the early-morning campfire. The previous day's journey had brought them to within smelling distance of the gold and O'Donnel wasn't going to let anything delay their departure.

Jim poured himself a mug of the strong beverage and hunkered down next to the big man. O'Donnel's silence had an almost companionable feel to it, all the more surprising when his silences were more usually the brooding sort.

'What's between you and Billy?' Jim took a chance on the big man answering. It was rare for O'Donnel to appear any more amiable than a grizzly bear guarding its young.

'He's a treacherous little swine and I don't trust him.' Jim already knew the ex-sergeant's opinion of Billy, but he wanted more. 'He's betrayed me before, when he cut and run at Petersburg. Johnny Wesson died there, died when Billy was supposed to give him covering fire. Most of our platoon died in that battle, and I damned near caught it too.'

'That isn't Billy's story,' Jim put in gently.

'Of course not! Billy's the hero of Petersburg if you believe his stories. According to him I was just a war-weary sergeant who risked his men's lives for the chance of personal glory.' O'Donnel sounded bitter. 'Not the only time he betrayed me either. We were in Madison once before, Billy and I. We robbed a bank to fund our own expedition into this god-forsaken wilderness. It was his damned stupid idea in the first place, but it might have worked. Only he'd already tipped off the sheriff.' O'Donnel laughed harshly. 'If the lawman hadn't been as crooked as Billy himself, he'd have put me out of the way and got the gold for himself. As it was Billy took a bullet in the gut and drew fifteen years' hard, same as me.'

'Do you suspect he's betrayed us?' Jim could see O'Donnel was leading up to something.

'Could be.' O'Donnel continued to stare into the fire. 'He slunk off to the saloon a couple of times while we were in Madison. I didn't pay it any mind at the time. Billy always did like a drink. I got to thinking lately, though. Billy's the most miserable coward I ever met, but he's treating this trip like a stroll on the deck of the *Mississippi Queen*. He's the only one of us who's not acting jumpy.'

'Perhaps he's anxious to get to the gold.'

'Or perhaps he's already sold us down the river. Fellow in Madison told me Holmes himself sometimes takes a drink in town.'

'Is that an accusation?' Jim watched Josh O'Donnel's face carefully.

'No. I've got no proof, not even enough of a suspicion to convince myself. I can't believe Billy thinks he's better off siding with Holmes, but I've still got a niggling feeling that something's wrong.'

'I'll scout out further today,' decided the gambler. 'If Holmes intends to pay us a visit, he'll have to act quick. The burned-out Confederate wagons can't be more than a few miles off if that map of Billy's is accurate.'

The pitiful remains of the wagon train proved easy to find. Just as Josh and Billy had foretold, they hadn't rotted away in the arid climate, though the ever encroaching sand was beginning to creep over their burned-out wells and bury the evidence of their violent history. Jim stood in his stirrups and stared moodily at the charred remains from a nearby promontory, perhaps the very hill that had sheltered Sergeant Donnel and his tiny troop of survivors all those years before. As they'd promised, a jagged ridge cut the horizon a few hundred yards beyond. Billy's story of untold riches looked like becoming fact.

He swivelled slowly, carefully surveying the sun-burned wilderness of sand and rugged spires of rock through his glass, stiffening when he spotted the tell-tale plume of dust. It rode the air like a banner, and spoke of a strong band of men riding hard. *We've been spotted*, he decided, and promptly urged his own mount into a run, heading back towards the oncoming wagons.

By the time the outlaw gang rode in the explorers had their wagons situated in a defensive position, hauled up in the lee of one of several rocky outcrops in the neighbourhood. Jim stood by the prow of the prairie wagon, his rifle at the slope, nonchalantly pulling on a cheroot, the thick, pungent black smoke coiling sinuously in the heavy air.

There were a score of outlaws in the group that pulled up to survey the scene, hauling on their reins just out of easy gunshot. Their leader, a swarthy individual dressed all in black, lean and cadaverous, with a livid scar sliced across his face to give the impression of a permanently malignant smile, stared at Jim through red-rimmed, expressionless eyes. He signalled the remainder of his troop to stay back and eased his horse into a slow trot, pushed back his wide-brimmed hat and held up one hand, palm outward, in the universal gesture of peace.

'You're trespassing on Mr Holmes's land, friend.' He didn't break his silence until he was looming over the gambler, his gravel-voiced opening speaking of something less than friendship.

Jim stared around the sterile wastes with an eloquent shrug and dismissed the messenger, certain in his own mind it wasn't the outlaw chief himself speaking. 'I don't see Zachariah Holmes complaining.'

'Do you know him?' The outlaw's black suiting didn't look so prepossessing close up. Both jacket and pants were stained and smeared with the evidence of long use, and the vest beneath was less dark than filthy.

'Only by reputation,' Jim replied to the question. He could see the other fancied himself as a gunman. In stark contrast to the rest of his raiment, his belt and holster were of oiled black leather, and the gun resting low on his thigh looked as though it was regularly and recently cleaned.

'Then you're a fool to pass by so close.'

Jim grinned, genuinely amused to be able to deliver such a bombshell to the outlaw. 'We're not passing through,' he told him. 'We planned to set up a travelling saloon. I'm sure you and your Comanchero friends would be glad of a fresh watering hole. We've got good liquor too, store bought from back East, not snake-eyed moonshine.'

The bait wasn't taken. The outlaw's face remained expressionless, and for a moment Jim was left abashed. Either his inquisitor held an icy control over his emotions, or he already suspected their enterprise. Had Billy said too much in a Madison saloon?

'Why don't we just take your liquor? Whole lot cheaper that way.' The black-clad Comanchero waved towards his waiting gang of desperadoes with a cocky grin on his face.

'Liquor's a lot more fun in a saloon,' Jim told him. 'We got a singer too. It'll be easier for both of us if you let us entertain you peaceably. Besides, I'm sure you don't want to get shot down attempting to rob us.'

'I'm not the one likely to get shot down.' His attempt at a triumphant smile, combined with the wicked scar and his snickering laughter to assume the form of a contorted grimace that made him look even more malignant.

Next moment the smile was wiped off his face and genuine surprise lit up his features. The sound of several rifles being cocked in swift succession had broken the desert silence. He looked up at the rocky outcrop that towered above them and slowly scanned the slopes. No fewer than a dozen rifle barrels had magically appeared and at least three heads were in full view.

'Tell Holmes I'd like to meet him personally,' Jim told the outlaw shortly. 'Perhaps he can see the advantages in our scheme.'

'No need for gunfire, friend.' The outlaw had changed his tune. 'Mr Holmes sent me down to escort you in. I hear you've got guns to trade too.'

Jim silently damned Billy for a blabbermouth. How much more did the Comancheros know about their expedition?

He nodded. 'We'll choose our own camp. I'd prefer to sleep easy.' He held out a hand to the still mounted outlaw.

The Comanchero studiously avoided the offer of friendship. 'The name's Riddick Tomms,' he told the gambler. 'Some people prefer to call me Black Riddick Tomms. Get your men down and follow me.' His slow, reptilian eyes flickered over the gambler.

Jim Murphy stared back, swiftly assessing the other's claims to be a gunman. Black Riddick Tomms had been a feared watchword amongst the inhabitants of Madison, second only to Holmes himself. He'd been accounted a killer, cold as ice and equipped with greased-lightning speed on the draw.

It was an assessment the gambler could readily accept now he'd seen the man.

Holmes had evidently already made his decision on their expedition and sent his lieutenant Tomms along to escort them. Nevertheless, Jim didn't want the outlaws to think they had it all their own way.

'I already scouted ahead,' he told the gunman easily. 'There's a parcel of burned-out wagons a mile or two out in that direction.' He indicated the narrow gap between two sun-baked spires of basalt that grew precipitously out of the desert sands. 'The ridge that overlooks them will provide some protection if the wind gets up. We'll make camp in its lee.'

'What if that's too far for us to visit regular?'

'Tough.' Jim had already decided from the other's tone that their suggested camp site wasn't too far from the gang's hideout. Neither would Holmes want them camping up close, not unless he planned to wipe them out later. He turned and signalled to the watchers on the hill.

Black Riddick Tomms watched the three of them emerge from their cover with an expressionless face, while they trailed down the steep hillside, each carrying a quartet of rifles.

'Clever,' he muttered. 'Are those the guns you got for sale?'

'Some of them,' confirmed Jim. 'There's a dozen,

in all, complete with ammunition.'

'We'll need more than that.'

'I'll take your orders and come back another time. A regular trip would make good sense for both parties. Fine liquor and a plentiful supply of guns. What more could a man want?'

'Women.'

'We'll bring some with us next time,' agreed the gambler equably.

'What about her?' Sera Angel McCall had reached the wagons, and even the mannish gear she'd adopted to undertake the tough trek couldn't disguise her femininity. Riddick Tomms's acquisitive gaze made it plain she was one extra he could settle for.

'She's just another barkeep,' Jim warned him. 'You might get the chance to hear her sing if you visit us of a night. Try to touch her and you'll be barred from being served.'

'Who'll stop me?' The outlaw's hand snaked down to touch his pistol with menacing precision.

'I will.' Josh O'Donnel had swapped the rifles for his favourite shotgun and pointed it directly at Riddick Tomms.

Tomms scowled. 'Ain't I seen you someplace?' Josh's bulk was a dead give-away, but Jim Murphy still hoped his clean shave might prove an effective enough disguise. After all, surely a man they'd captured before wouldn't put his head back in the noose.

'I reckon I'd recognize a skunk like you, if we'd ever met before,' returned Josh unsmilingly. He kept the shotgun trained on the gunman's midriff until the other turned his mount away.

The four companions reached their intended campsite well before noon, keeping their wagons in close-up formation in case Black Riddick Tomms changed his mind once he was out of gunshot range.

'Where now?' Jim had swapped his saddle for a place alongside Josh on the massive prairie wagon, with his mount made fast to its tailgate. They'd reached the burned-out wagons and he scanned the big man's face anxiously, wondering whether he could truly have memorized the intricacies of a chart, which was itself only drawn from memory.

'Over there.' Josh O'Donnel was as economical with his words as ever, but apparently sure of his directions. Then, in an uncharacteristically loquacious manner. 'I've been waiting for this moment for close on twenty-five years. I could lead you direct to the gold even without the aid of a map.' He lashed the leaders back into life and turned the team in the direction of the nearby crumbling cliff faces. 'How close can we get?'

'Close as you like,' Jim replied. 'Gold's heavy. No

sense in carrying it too far. More chance of being spotted if we do.'

'If them outlaws are suspicious, they'll be watching us. Setting up camp too close to the spot might give the secret away.'

'If they're suspicious, then we're dead meat anyway,' the gambler replied. 'They won't allow you to escape them twice.' He stared at the big man suspiciously. 'How close were you when they captured you last time?'

'We were barely a day off Madison.' Josh O'Donnel looked serious. 'They hit us without warning, but they knew what they were looking for.' He thought back on his lucky escape and grunted. 'Me. The others were gunned down without any ceremony.' He pulled the wagon to a halt and gestured to the stark and empty country about them. 'We've arrived.'

Jim stared around him. On one side the desert rolled out flat as far as the horizon, its monotonous landscape interrupted here and there by the rocky outcrops and huge basaltic columns through which they'd wended their way. On the other ran the ridge, stretching out in a more or less straight line as far he could see. He was educated enough to know it must trace the course of an old fault line, but he didn't waste his time on such fripperies. Small landslides such as Billy had described as burying the gold seemed to be common along its length, and there were at least three in close proximity to their position.

'Are you sure?' he queried. 'It all looks alike to me.'

'It's there for sure.' Josh nodded towards the nearest pile of rocks, not daring to point when their outlaw escort was still trailing in their wake. 'Or perhaps there.' He too stared at the jumbled, sun-fried rock. He was in the right place, that much he was sure of, but he'd somehow expected their rock fall to have been as raw and new as when they'd triggered it. Time had evidently healed the wounds, the searing bleach of the sun working alongside the all too frequent sandstorms to obscure the freshness of the landslip.

'We'd better get set to make a night of it.' Jim slipped off his high perch with athletic ease and called in Billy's wagon to make camp alongside the prairie wagon. 'This lot will be parched and anxious to steal a march on their fellow Comancheros.'

CHAPTER EIGHT

THE GOLD CAMP

'This will do us,' Jim told Riddick Tomms when he rode up to find out why they'd stopped.

Tomms glanced around the site with a faintly bemused air, then turned his malignant gaze back on the gambler.

'What if it ain't convenient?'

'It's convenient enough for us,' replied Jim decisively. He'd been watching the remainder of the escorting outlaws and had formed a distinct impression that their camp was closer than Riddick Tomms was prepared to admit. 'You wouldn't want us to end up camping on your doorstep and risk a posse following in our tracks.'

'It'd take an army to winkle us out of these hills,' boasted the gunman. 'Stay if you want, it's all the same to me.'

It wasn't all the same to Tomms, though. A gambling man had to be capable of reading the signs, and something in the way he held himself told Jim the gunman was dissembling. He wanted them to set up camp right here, or close by, at any rate. Would probably have forced the matter if they didn't. Did he have his own reasons? Perhaps at an order from his boss. Or was there something else? His whole attitude had suggested triumph, but he'd been puzzled too. Come to that, where was his boss? Holmes hadn't gained his fearsome reputation by taking a back seat when action was demanded. Or was a mere travelling saloon beneath his notice? Jim gave up trying to analyse the whole damned shebang. They were situated where they wanted to be, and whether that was for good or for bad could safely be left for fate to decide.

'Free drinks all round,' he called out for the benefit of the other Comancheros, who immediately slipped out of their saddles with a whoop of triumph. 'Billy, Sera. Set them up.'

'How long will it take you to find the gold?' Jim drew Josh to one side, ostensibly to begin work on unloading the wagon. Part of the cargo consisted of a temporary bar counter which they could erect along the side of the prairie wagon. 'It doesn't look an easy job.'

'You're right there,' Josh agreed disconsolately. 'We must be close by, though. We'll search those old rock falls one by one until we find it.' He stared at the crumbling piles of dislodged rock, narrowing his eyes as though he could bore through the cliffs by sheer force of will. Then he transferred his attention to the outlaws gathered around the back of Billy's wagon with a dissatisfied expression on his face. 'We'll start as soon as they leave.'

As it happened, there was no opportunity that day to begin their search. Most of the outlaws they'd already met were quite content to remain by the wagons, drinking and carousing all afternoon. Towards evening other groups of desperadoes began to trickle in and by the time night had fallen there must have been forty of the Comanchero gang in residence.

While Billy and Sera continued to serve from the makeshift bar, Josh and Jim set up a temporary forge under cover of providing a fire, made up from the charred timbers of the old Confederate wagons, against the chill of a desert night. The huge bellows, still hidden under tarpaulin inside the wagon, would require more explanation than they were prepared to offer at the moment, but that wouldn't be needed until they found the golden ingots.

Most of the outlaws were interested in acquiring guns and ammunition, and an impromptu sale netted the small band of entrepreneurs a tidy profit on the armaments they had brought. To add authenticity to their role, Jim also took orders for additional items, promising to return with them within the month.

The scene was one of celebration and Jim found himself thoroughly satisfied with the progress they'd made. The Comancheros turned out to be friendly in the main, in stark contrast to Riddick Tomms's attitude, and behaved with as much propriety as could be expected from a bunch of lawless desperadoes. They drank heavily, whooped, sang and even brawled, but never with any deliberately vicious intent.

Sera changed into a low-cut gown later in the evening and, preparing to use the tailboard of Billy's wagon as an impromptu stage, steeled herself to entertain the rough and ready crowd.

'And now.' Billy elected himself as master of ceremonies. 'Direct from the Mississippi showboats, I give you' – his voice rose into a positive roar – 'Miss Sera Angel McCall.'

Sera appeared from behind the canvas covering to a positive maelstrom of applause and raucous whistling. Once the noise had died down her first number was sung slowly and with feeling. Jim Murphy was inclined to question whether her dress was too revealing at first, but was relieved to find the ragtag clientele, wanted for murder and mayhem all across the west, were quite content to lounge comfortably around the campsite and listen to the pretty songbird. Sera's high, clear voice extracted every ounce of sentiment from an old tear-jerker and the air was completed in a hush.

The girl was good, Jim admitted. She really could sing, not just hold a tune, and she presented well too, enlivening her performance with huge personality. Too talented to spend her life in cheap, Western saloons, he decided; not that she'd ever need to perform again once they'd carted off the gold.

Having silenced the tough desperadoes with her artistry, the girl abruptly changed tempo. Swirling her skirts with artful, mesmeric intent, she swung into an old Civil War melody, prancing about the makeshift stage while she exhorted the men to sing along with her. A soft lullaby, crooned as though each of the audience was the only man there; a love song that held them spellbound; and half a dozen others before she held out a dainty hand to be helped down from the high-lodged tailgate.

Sera gracefully thanked the man whose hand she'd grasped for support and sashayed alluringly across to the makeshift bar, where several of the outlaws jostled for the honour of paying for her drink.

'Congratulations,' Jim told her when he passed yet another shot of rye across the bar top to her. 'At this rate, we'll have a full house every night.'

'Long as they leave by midnight,' she told him warmly, 'every outlaw in the territory is welcome.' She turned to thank her latest companion and allowed him to kiss her hand. 'I'll do my share of the bar work too,' she told Jim, 'but I'll get changed first.'

Like most of the men there, Jim watched Sera walk off towards the wagon she'd so recently performed upon. The way her hips undulated under the thin cloth of her gown was a performance in itself and the gambler found himself reacting in a way he seldom did around a woman these days. *She's trouble*, he told himself, but he refused to listen, only watched while she swung herself up on to the open tailgate and slipped out of sight behind the thick wall of canvas stretched across the well of the wagon.

Black Riddick Tomms, the Comanchero's leader, had disappeared too, Jim realized with a sudden start. Some latent instinct, long buried in his subconscious, told him where the man could be found. He'd seen the outlaw ogling Sera during her performance and swiftly extrapolated the facts.

It was the work of a moment to stride over to the

wagon, leap on the tailgate and tear back the canvas. Sera was forced back against a stack of wooden boxes, a knife at her throat to keep her quiet while Tomms pawed at the neckline to her gown.

'Get out,' he growled, evidently understanding that someone was behind him, but too intent on his own dirty work to waste time in discovering the intruder's identity. He tore down and the material ripped.

'Get out yourself.' Jim caught the outlaw by the back of his collar and swung him around, yanking him roughly towards the entrance.

'Damn you for a—' Riddick Tomms went for his gun, but both his speedy draw and his words were interrupted by the flying fist that connected with his jaw. If he hadn't already been teetering on the edge of the wagon, things might have gone badly for the gambler, but as it was the deadly pistol flew from the outlaw's grasp when he fell headlong off the tailgate.

The drop was too short to injure him, but it knocked the breath out of his lungs. Before he recovered his wits enough to scrabble around for his gun the gambler had followed him out of the vehicle and kicked it away.

Though he'd been tempted to shoot the outlaw out of hand, Jim had quickly realized how unwise resorting to gunplay would be. The heavy drinking band of Comancheros would sanction a fist fight, especially once they realized their songstress had been attacked by Tomms, but they'd react violently to his shooting Holmes's trusted lieutenant.

Tomms rose to his feet and angrily rushed the gambler, who calmly stood aside and rattled in a tattoo of punches to the other's head. Tomms turned again, a bull at bay, but gave ground when Jim stepped forward and unleashed a barrage of punches that left his opponent swaying.

For a moment it looked as though the fight was over, but Tomms was a violent man, used to rough-house fights. He switched tactics abruptly, kicked out at his opponent's shin to gain a breathing space and, realizing that the gambler had the skill to beat him to the punch, bored in to take the fight to close quarters.

Jim rattled his rib cage before the gunman managed to take a grip, but had to give way when Tomms thudded into him and began to gouge at his eyes. In return Jim tore at the gunman's over-long, greasy hair and was rewarded with a howl of agony when the heel of his hand slammed painfully into Tomms's nose. As the outlaws began to gather around, the two men staggered back and forth, each unsuccessfully trying to gain a telling advantage over the other. And though he wasn't aware of it at the time, many of them were shouting for Jim Murphy to win.

So far as size and strength went, the fighters were evenly matched, but they fought with distinctly different styles. The gambler's furious onslaught had swiftly been tempered by an icy composure which slowly but surely gave him the edge, while the gunman's vicious assaults were fed on pure aggression.

Both men were tired, but neither could afford to present the other with an opening. The ring of applauding onlookers had drawn closer as the adversaries slowed, their breath coming in awkward gasps while they struggled against one another. Jim gave back suddenly, momentarily unbalancing the gunman, allowing him the space to slice in a hook to Tomms's short ribs, stopping the man in his tracks.

The gambler realized this was his chance. He took it with alacrity. A right swing, which Tomms should have evaded with ease, took him on the point of his jaw and he dropped to his knees. Jim was in no mood to be merciful. He followed up his advantage, driving blow after blow into his opponent's bloody mask of a face.

'That's enough, Jim.' Josh, shotgun in hand, stopped him at last, and Tomms sank to the ground, beaten and exhausted.

Jim himself staggered, but recovered swiftly, surprised at how calmly the outlaws accepted that their leader had been beaten. Black Riddick Tomms wasn't a popular man, then, but evidently a dangerous one, and Jim surreptitiously kicked the outlaw's pistol into the darker shadows under one of the wagons. He was in no mood to be shot in the back.

'Will you take a drink with me?' Sera appeared with a bottle and a couple of shot glasses in one hand and a wet towel in the other. Leading him out of the direct glare of the fire, she sat him on a conveniently flat, wind-scoured boulder and began to bathe his cuts.

The outlaws drifted back to their drinking, laughing and belching around the makeshift bar. The fight had been over the woman, and they were as content to let Jim enjoy the spoils as they would have allowed their own man.

'Thank you for intervening, Jim.' Sera's face was still pale after the shock of her ordeal, but she toasted the gambler gratefully once she'd splashed generous portions of the potent spirit into their glasses. 'I was scared stiff of him, but maybe you shouldn't have interfered. Riddick Tomms is a dangerous man for anyone to make an enemy of. They say he's pure poison on the draw.'

Jim knew that much already. It was only luck that his punch had jolted Tomms off the wagon and caused him to drop the pistol he'd drawn so adroitly.

'They're all dangerous,' he warned her. 'There's

not one of them would hesitate to shoot his own grandmother for a few lousy cents.'

'They've behaved like proper gentlemen towards me,' she teased. 'One of them even complimented me on my appearance.' She'd pinned up her torn bodice, but switched her hips until her skirts flared out in the hopes of securing another compliment.

'You're an artist,' conceded Jim, 'but if any one of them ever caught you alone, especially in that dress, you'd soon see them revert to type. Riddick Tomms is no different from the next man.'

'Did you like my costume?' Sera struck a pose and abruptly changed the subject.

'That's not the point.'

'Whatever do you mean?' She spun around on the spot, allowing her hemline to float on the air, and decided she liked flirting with Jim.

'It's not appropriate out here,' he responded curtly, but there was a predatory gleam in his eyes that the girl judged to be approval.

'Anything that keeps their attention away from what we're really doing out here is appropriate,' she replied seriously. Then, of a sudden, she leaned forward and kissed him full on the lips. 'I'll go change.' She laughed, and danced away with a cheeky grin on her face.

CHAPTER NINE

IN THE PRESENCE
OF WEALTH

The outlaws continued to carouse until way past midnight, when Jim eventually decided to shut up shop.

'Come back tomorrow evening and we'll open up again,' he told them. 'We need our sleep and so do you.'

'We need a drink, more like,' one of them struck back, his words slurred almost beyond understanding.

'You'd never stop drinking.' Jim grinned, twirling the man around and shoving him off towards his mount.

'There's a couple more over here,' warned Sera.

She stared at the unconscious men and curled her lip disdainfully. 'They're dead drunk. No point in trying to set them on a horse.'

'We'll settle them under one of the wagons,' Jim decided, idly waving off the last of the mounted outlaws. 'Josh,' he called. 'Give me a hand, and then Sera can tuck them in with a blanket.' He surveyed the sorry remains of the outlaws' revelry: three men who wouldn't be riding this side of dawn.

'We can't go out exploring while they're sleeping it off,' Billy complained angrily. 'Damn fool idea to let them drink so much.'

'Billy's right for once.' Josh stared at the gambler for leadership. 'If they spot us exploring the cliffs, they'll soon latch on to our real aim.'

'They're drunk as skunks,' Jim assured him. 'Even if they do wake up before morning, they'll be too hung-over to worry about what we're doing.' He drew his companions far enough from the drunken men to ensure no chance remark could be overheard. 'We've got until sunup to find our landslide,' he told them. 'It's not worth our while searching past daylight. If Holmes has any suspicions at all, he'll have someone watching.'

'He may be out there himself right now.' Josh O'Donnel stared suspiciously out into the surrounding darkness.

'He won't see anything if he is,' responded the

gambler confidently. 'It's an almost new moon, barely enough light for us to start searching, let alone spot anyone from a distance.'

'We'll need more light to dig.' Josh surveyed the nearest pile of crumbling rocks dismally.

'We don't need to start digging yet,' Jim reminded the big ex-sergeant gently. 'It'd take us weeks to excavate even the nearer rock falls.' He indicated the disintegrating line of the ridge.

'Then. . . ?'

'When Billy told me about the site, he described it as a narrow canyon, the entrance to which was sealed when you deliberately started the landslide to hide the gold.'

'True enough.' The big ex-sergeant stared at the gambler.

'That being so, the canyon itself must still exist and any fall from solid cliff can be dismissed.'

'This one looks pretty solid to me.' Josh stalked across to the nearest pile of boulders, a mere twenty or thirty yards from the camp, and stared up at the cliffs above.

'Seems like it,' Jim agreed, but he surveyed the rugged pile of boulders with misgiving. 'We've got to thoroughly explore each and every one of these falls in case there's a hidden void.'

'Tom's map was pretty clear. It must be close at hand.'

'Maybe.' Jim's tone was less sure than that of the big ex-sergeant. 'He drew it from memory and that can play tricks on you. Only thing we're sure about is the burned-out wagons, which put us in the right area. Given that, the gold could be anywhere within half a mile of here.' He stopped and thought for a moment. 'We'll split up and divide the labour,' he decided. 'Josh, you and Billy work your way north. Sera and I'll head in the opposite direction.' He stared at the crumbling rocks with distaste. 'Don't take any chances,' he warned, 'and make sure you're back in camp by sunup.'

The rising sun found them dirty and exhausted, with nothing more than cuts and bruises to show for their pains. And the next few days followed the same unchanging pattern: sleeping until late in the day; collecting wood from the remnants of the burned-out wagons to feed the fire; serving and entertaining their thirsty Comanchero customers; and ending by conducting yet another unsuccessful night search of the crumbling cliff face.

'It must be somewhere around here.' Josh stuck his head in his hands late one afternoon. 'Tom's map, my own memories. They all coincide, but we've searched every inch of this cliff within a half-mile without striking a clue.'

'Then we search again, more thoroughly,' Jim told

him, 'and keep on searching until we find it. The moon's waxing, so the light should be good tonight.' He stared around the desert wilderness, checking out the jumble of hills and cliffs that might hide any guard Holmes had set over them.

Not that either of them had any reason to suspect that they were being watched. They'd seen neither hide nor hair of the feared outlaw chief since their arrival, and even his lieutenant, Black Riddick Tomms, seemed to have disappeared. Not that his absence caused them any grief.

'Where's Sera?' Jim changed the subject abruptly. 'She can go with me to pack some wood before we run out of fuel for the fire.'

'I haven't seen her since this morning,' admitted Josh sleepily.

'She went scouting out down one of those little side canyons north of here,' mumbled Billy. 'Looking for some old dry brush for the fire. I told her I'd seen some.'

'How long, Billy?' Jim narrowed his eyes against the glare of the afternoon sun. They were sitting in the shade of a tarpaulin stretched out between the two wagons; outside it would hot enough a fry a man's brain. A stray gust of the ever present wind blew a cloud of stinging dust into his eyes.

'Hours, since. You'd think she'd be back by now.'

Billy didn't seem bothered by the girl's

disappearance, but Josh joined Jim in staring along the line of the cliff.

'No sign of her,' he ventured. 'Do you think she's lost her way?'

'More likely she's taken a fall,' Jim returned, a sense of foreboding tugging at his breast. 'I'll scout out and see if I can find her.' He turned towards Billy. 'Where's this canyon of yours?'

'It's only a couple of hundred yards away, but you can't see the opening until you're on top of it. Set off north and it's in plain view. Sera can't have failed to spot it. It's a dead end too, so she can't lose herself.'

Josh nodded. 'I know the spot. The opening sort of doubles back on itself. I didn't see any brush, though. Nor anything else, other than sun-blasted rock. If Sera really has gone up there exploring, she'll be easy to find. It's little more than a hole in the cliff face.'

'I'll check it out while you two wait here. No sense in having all four of us scattered around this god-damned wilderness.'

Jim picked up his rifle and set out, finding the canyon as easy to locate as Billy had suggested, and as empty as Josh had foretold. Puzzled by the girl's continued disappearance, the gambler began to study the sandy canyon floor. He had no skill as a tracker, but surely a footprint. . . ? He grunted angrily and turned his attention to the rocky slopes above; the wind whirled around the narrow canyon, plucking up little sand devils that covered his own prints as fast as they were made.

He attempted to shout. 'Sera.' The sound echoed around the little box canyon, but didn't bring an answer from the girl.

Billy was right about the brush, though. A small heap of sun-bleached twigs that looked as old as the hills lay in a far corner of the canyon, and even as he watched, a stray gust of wind lifted and scattered them. Sera had been here! She must have gathered the brush and left it there; it would never have collected naturally in such an exposed position.

Jim strode across and stared at the evidence. His eyes rose and followed the path revealed. The cliff could be climbed by way of a natural fault line that had weathered faster than the surrounding rock. Sera must have scrambled up it, but why? He looked around, half-expecting to find the reason, only to remain disappointed. If there was any point to her madness, then it was invisible to him. He took a further moment to to make his decision before he laid aside his rifle and started to clamber up the steep incline himself.

From the top for as far as he could see lay a wild, desolate, arid landscape: tall rocky spires merging with barren sands and sun-wasted cliffs marching across the empty desert. If Sera was out there, then she was lost, and he felt again the unfamiliar tug at his heart.

A bird floated into his sight, spiralling down from out of the gleaming copper sky. A big bird, a carrion eater, and Jim Murphy knew what it had spotted. He settled back, determined not to disturb the creature until he had its direction. It must have located Sera from its lofty patrol, and it would lead him to her just as surely. It glided out of sight, dropping into yet another hidden canyon in the hills, and Jim set out to follow it, steeling himself to finding no more than her body.

By the time he'd discovered its landing ground, the lean shape of the vulture was waddling awkwardly across the flat, stony canyon floor towards a shadowed cavern in the canyon wall. A slim, shapely arm emerged to wave vigorously, and it retreated, its beady eyes anxiously assessing its intended prey's capacity to resist. Jim, helpless from above, could only toss rocky chippings at its scrawny frame, but he took heart when it flapped its wings, lumbered into an ungainly take-off and struggled into the rising currents with rapidly beating wings. It screamed out a feral challenge, perhaps a promise to return and dine off both of them, for Jim could see no easy path down the precipitous cliffs.

'Be careful, Jim.' Sera, alerted to his arrival by the stones he'd thrown, emerged from her shelter to issue a warning. 'Don't come down, it's too dangerous. That cliff's treacherous.'

The warning was unnecessary in the circumstances. Jim could clearly see the livid bruise that marked her forehead, with blood still welling slowly from the contusion at its centre, and he had no intention of leaving her to her own devices. He started the climb with care, testing every foothold before he trusted it with his weight, but in the end his descent was every bit as scrambled as hers had evidently been. About halfway down, he began to slide, clutching vainly at the friable rock, until in the end he tumbled all of twenty feet. Fortunately the floor was covered in soft sand at the point of impact, deep enough to break his fall, and he took no more harm than a couple of bruises.

Sera rushed to his side, her concern mirrored in her eyes. 'Jim,' she cried and flung her arms around him.

'Sera,' he whispered tenderly, holding her close, glorying in the sensations of her body crushed hard against his own. Then, realizing where they were. 'What the devil are you doing down here?'

'Riddick Tomms.' Sera told him, extricating herself from his embrace to stare around the canyon's rim. 'I saw him.'

'Where?' Jim took out his pistol and followed her gaze.

'I went to collect brushwood, but he must have been watching.' She rose lithely to her feet. 'I was in a box canyon with only one entrance, and he was blocking it. I shrank back into a corner and spotted my escape, enough handholds to climb the cliff, but he was after me and I had to flee. I tried to hide, but took a tumble instead.' She dashed away the blood from her head. 'I think I might have been knocked unconscious when I fell.'

Riddick Tomms! Jim's eyes searched around the cliffs above; they were in a natural bowl, dug out of the rock and super-heated by the merciless sun. There was no cover, and if Tomms were up there and spotted their plight, they'd be sitting ducks.

'When I woke up I found myself in this blank canyon with no way out. I saw the cave over there,' she pointed out a shadowed opening, 'though it's more like a gap between two large boulders, and I hid. I was frightened that Tomms would follow me down if he found me.'

'Not much chance of that,' Jim allowed. 'He could search for a year and not discover this place.' Despite his confident assurances, the gambler didn't replace his own pistol in its holster; he might not have been the only one to follow the vulture's flight.

'There's a metal box in there too.' Sera held the gambler's eye. 'It's trapped under a rock fall, so it can't be moved.'

'The gold,' breathed Jim. He strode over to the cramped confines of the little cavern and peered into its depths. There was a box there, low and wide, tucked under the crushing weight of the solid rock above. It was as grey and filthy as the ground it rested on, but undeniably the sort of container Josh and Billy had buried all those years before.

He knelt in the restricted space and tugged on the box, working his hand under its edge to get a grip. It wouldn't budge, but he had another trick up his sleeve. He began to dig away the sandy deposits of the canyon floor beneath the box with his knife. A few minutes later he had his answer; the box slid neatly out of its hiding-place, minus its lid which had stuck fast on the rock above. It was full of golden bars, as shiny as when new.

Sera breathed an earthy curse and reached out to touch the precious metal. 'This is where they hid it,' she muttered with almost reverential awe.

'Have you recovered far enough to climb?' Jim suddenly returned from the euphoric to the prosaic. The gold was of no earthly use to anyone if they were stuck in a hole with no food and precious little water. He stared the girl in the eye wondering about the after-effects of her fall. He wasn't an expert, but it didn't look as if she was suffering from concussion. Nevertheless, any exercise in this climate would be hard following such traumatic experiences.

'I'm ready,' she replied courageously, her eyes still on the golden hoard, 'but I don't see how.'

The gambler backed out of the cavern and searched around the precipitous cliffs that hemmed them in, swiftly discovering the weakest point.

'Up there.' He pointed out a route that led them directly over the cavern's entrance, through a jumble of rock that had evidently collapsed from above at some time in the recent past. 'It's loose scree and jagged boulders for the most part,' he opined. 'There'll be gaps enough to provide us with footholds.' He picked up a gold ingot and thrust it securely through his belt.

In the end the route proved ridiculously easy. As he'd foreseen, the boulders had crashed down from the higher slopes above at some recent date, probably overlaying the landslide Sergeant O'Donnel and his men had engineered so many years before. The wind had blown the dusty desert sand into the cavities, but, although the work was taxing, it hadn't yet hardened to a consistency that prevented them from digging it out to provide a secure hold for their hands and feet. Twenty minutes later they were atop the cliffs overlooking their own campsite. The landslide this side of the hill had flung debris far out on to the desert floor and was relatively easy to pick their way through. Considering its extent, it was small wonder they hadn't considered it worth exploring further.

CHAPTER TEN

ZACHARIAH HOLMES UNCOVERED

There was much for the four companions to do before they could set out to recover the gold. For starters, a desperate bunch of outlaws would soon be riding in, anxious to get down to some serious drinking and to catch another of Sera's popular performances.

Jim barely had a chance to do more than show Josh and Billy the single gold bar he'd rescued before the Comancheros rode in, but the mood that night was one of unusual euphoria.

Party over, Jim shut up the bar, and the happy

band began to put into place the plans they'd already prepared. The rear wheels on the big prairie wagon were dismantled on the pretext of a broken axle, to mend which they'd need the fire building up and the huge bellows installed. It took them most of the night, but by the time morning came, the huge axle had been bent out of true across the fire to provide convincing visual evidence for their lie.

'We'll have to risk recovering the gold during daylight hours,' Jim decided once they'd all gathered by the huge landslide after a few hours of badly needed sleep. 'The whole slope's too unstable to work by night.'

'We didn't create this nightmare.' Josh shook his head, appalled by the tons of shattered rock in front of him. 'It wouldn't have taken more than a few hours to clear the debris we left.'

'A second landslide,' the gambler hazarded. 'May have lain here for years, but there's no point trying to hack our way through it. It'd take a team of navvies working with explosives to blast a path through that lot.' He spoke directly to Josh O'Donnel. 'Were all the boxes close together?'

'We packed them in rows, three or four deep,' confirmed the big ex-sergeant. 'Must have been twenty or more, each holding a dozen gold bars.'

'Then we'll find them packed in the ground behind the cave,' Jim told them confidently. 'Long as we're careful and pack supports to hold the rocks above, I don't see why we shouldn't be able to reach most of the gold.'

'How do we get it out?'

Jim pointed up the slope. 'There's a natural ridge up top, out of sight from the wagons. It's solid rock, not part of the slide, so it ought to be firm enough to construct a hoist on. Once we've extracted the gold, we can haul it up piecemeal and pack it down the slope this side by hand. That'll be backbreaking work, but I don't see any alternative.'

'When do we start?'

'Right now.' Jim grinned enthusiastically. 'We'll get cracking on the hoist first.' He pointed out Josh as his companion. 'Billy and Sera can fetch timber from the burned-out wagons, anything will do. We'll use the heavier pieces to support the roof of the cave and the rest, however charred, can go on the fire. Any gold we recover must be melted down before we open the saloon of an evening. Once those Comancheros get a whiff of gold in their nostrils we can say goodbye to our chances of escape.'

The next few days saw the little party working around the clock, recovering and salting away the gold one bar at a time.

Jim became their miner, perilously delving deeper and deeper beneath the shifting mass of the landslide, and shoring up the unstable rock with hand-made supports that creaked and groaned under the weight of stone above. Billy handled the hoist, dragging the heavy metal up the sheer sides of the boxed-in canyon, while Josh used his massive strength to transport the gold back to their base by the wagons. There, Sera sweated over the makeshift forge, melting gold bar after gold bar into the vats they'd brought with them. And there too, Josh would join her in pouring the molten liquid into the grooves they'd sliced into the metal underpinnings of the wagons.

Their work ended on the stroke of midday, despite Billy's constant complaints that it was safe to continue. The entire site had to be tidied and made ready for the outlaws to descend on them for the evening revels, and the gold had to be cool enough for its presence to be disguised with liberal dollops of axle grease.

Then one day the situation changed with a suddenness that startled them all.

It was early, with dawn still staining the desert sky a delicate pink, when four men rode in. The four companions were already up and about, preparing themselves for another hard day's work, and Jim, who was busily spooning breakfast down his throat, stood up to greet them.

'Gilt Bartram.' The tone of his voice announced

his amazement. 'What are you. . . ?' He didn't finish the question. What Gilt was doing became obvious when Jim recognized his companions. One of them was Black Riddick Tomms, and all four men hefted rifles in a way that suggested they meant business.

'What is it, Gilt? I didn't realize you needed money bad enough to team up with a blackguard like Tomms.' Jim thought he understood the situation, but events swiftly proved him wrong.

'Shall I get their guns, Mr Holmes.' It was Billy speaking and all three of his companions stared at him in astonishment.

'Thank you, Billy.' Gilt Bartram grinned at the expression on Jim's face. 'He's right,' he confirmed. 'I am Zachariah Holmes and Billy's been working for me.'

'More fool him.' Jim allowed Billy to take his pistol and the knife he kept in a scabbard at the back of his belt. 'How long have you known?'

'Billy's been here before, Jim,' explained Gilt with a confident smile. 'We caught him sneaking into the desert and beat the truth out of him. Found the wagons where they always were, but he couldn't locate the gold. He swore he'd bring me the other map, so I let him go.' He laughed, but there was no mirth reflected in his eyes. 'I must have been in a good mood that day.'

'You'd have let that drummer kill him in New

Orleans.' Jim remembered the incident well. He tried to keep his eyes off Billy, grinding his teeth in silent helplessness while the treacherous little man searched Sera for her tiny derringer, allowing his hands to linger lovingly on her curves.

Gilt Bartram shrugged. 'The little weasel hadn't delivered. He was no use to me, until I discovered he was cosying up to you. I'd already marked out O'Donnel as the man to kidnap and torture into speaking, but he's a stubborn man, and there's no telling that he wouldn't have died first. You're mighty good at persuading people, and I thought with your help he might be brought round to lead us to the gold willingly. Everyone on the river knows you're as honest as the day's long, and he'd trust you where he wouldn't me, nor Billy either. You're a clever man too, it was inventive of you to devise a method to sneak the gold out from under my very nose. I can appreciate your techniques. Using them might allow me to evade awkward questions from the law too.'

'I've got them all, Mr Holmes.' Billy interrupted their tête à tête. He'd evidently stripped Josh of his armament too, and he displayed his prizes for the outlaw leader's benefit.

'Throw them on the wagon, Billy – your own weapons too.' Bartram's rifle centred on Billy's chest.

'No.' Billy looked horrified. 'I did all you asked of

me, Mr Holmes. I told you right away when we found the gold. You promised me a share.' He risked a sidelong glance at his former comrades. Josh O'Donnel glared back as though he'd be happy to tear his head off his shoulders, and neither of the others looked as though they'd stop him doing just that.

'I can't abide sharing with the likes of you.' Gilt Bartram urged his horse forward and kicked Billy viciously in the face. 'Get those guns secured,' he told Riddick Tomms urgently.

'How long have you led these outlaws?' Jim posed the question.

'I was born Zachariah Holmes,' Gilt admitted. 'Not quite the Southern gentleman I sought to be, my family were dirt poor, but I fought as hard as anyone for the Confederacy. Then them damned carpetbaggers took what little I had off me, so I gathered an army together to avenge myself.

'To start with they were mostly ex-Confederates down on their luck, but our reputation soon began to attract every thief and murderer in the county. We hit those damned Yankees everywhere it hurt: banks, trains, stagecoaches, anything that paid us a dime.' He laughed again, confident he had his audience. 'My share gave me enough to play the gentleman and live off the fat of the land instead of residing with the thieves and killers I led. I stole the name off one of my victims, along with his watch.' He took out the ornate fob watch Jim had seen so many times before and read the name inscribed in its case. ' "Gilt Bartram." It has a ring to it. A real Southern gentleman.'

'You were still an outlaw,' Jim reminded him flatly.

'I would have left the gang to its own devices if it hadn't been for the gold. Owning that would' – he corrected himself – '*will* allow me to buy up a fine Southern estate and take my position in the most refined of society. I may even rate the rank of colonel.' He struck a pose. 'Colonel Bartram, ex-stalwart of the Confederate army. Good old Gilt to his friends.'

'What about your companions?'

'Riddick Tomms will be my overseer in the fields. He's a brutal man, and a job like that will suit him.' He lowered his voice so only Jim could hear his chilling admission. 'The other two are simply the tools I have to use. I'll shoot them down once I'm through with them.'

'What about us?'

'You'll die too,' Gilt Bartram promised. 'A great pity,' he admitted sadly. 'I always liked you, Jim. You were good with the cards too. I might have thrown in with you myself, if I hadn't realized you were an honest man.'

'I expect I'd have ended up dead, just like your

other employees are due to.'

'How well you've come to know me,' admitted Bartram. 'I never could bear to share anything, even when I was young. Especially money.'

'What now?'

'You work for us. If you bring in the rest of the gold peaceable then I'll see you die easy. If not,' he shrugged, 'Riddick has some awful bad habits, and a way with a knife he learned from the Indians.'

'We'll work,' Jim decided and flung a fulminating glare towards Josh, who looked more likely to throw himself on the outlaw leader there and then. That would be suicidal and they both knew it.

'Get off me!'

Jim's brows drew together as Riddick Tomms caught hold of the struggling form of Sera and began to fondle her.

'Leave the girl alone,' Gilt had seen the expression on the gambler's face and, seeking to avoid unnecessary trouble, flung the command at his lieutenant. 'The gold comes first, and she's here to work as hard as any of them.'

'Aren't you afraid your Comancheros will want to be cut in for a share?' Jim asked, fighting to rein in his anger. 'When they arrive tonight and find you holding us they'll demand an explanation. They're not all as stupid as Tomms, and they won't enjoy being double-crossed.'

'I've arranged a little diversion for them,' Gilt explained smoothly. 'They won't be returning here for two or three days. and we'll be long gone by then.'

'Yeah.' Riddick Tomms thrust his face into the gambler's and sneered. 'You can open the bar for just us four tonight, while your lady friend sings for our entertainment.' He laughed coarsely, enjoying himself at Jim's expense. 'Soon as we got the gold, she'll be offering me a private performance, less formal without her clothes on. 'Course, you won't see that – I'm gonna gun you down soon as Mr Holmes has finished with you.'

CHAPTER ELEVEN

FIGHTING BACK

The work didn't change with Gilt Bartram in charge, the hours just got longer. Jim and Josh were set to work together at the bottom of the canyon, tunnelling deeper under the rocks to get at the remainder of the golden hoard, while Sera and Billy would labour up and down the slopes with the heavy ingots under close guard from Black Riddick Tomms. Bartram evidently considered recovering the gold more important than hiding it; melting it down for carrying away was a secondary consideration, to be completed at his leisure.

With the remaining gold buried deep beneath the rock fall and much harder to get at, some little time passed before Jim could dig his way through to the next box. With Josh stretched out on his belly behind the gambler and passing through the timber needed to shore up the rocks above, the guards began to get bored and complacent, lounging comfortably close together on a rocky ledge a dozen feet above the miners. They were packing rifles and evidently considered themselves safe enough from the two men toiling underground.

'Do you think you can haul out that big boulder?' Jim whispered when at last he eased himself out of the hole with a couple of sparkling gold bars in his arms and held them up to show the guards.

Josh rapidly surveyed the flat section of a huge rock directly under the guard's position. 'It won't be easy,' he murmured out the corner of his mouth, 'but I can make the attempt.'

'You'll only get one chance,' warned the gambler. 'If you fail, they'll either shoot you outright, or make sure they never put themselves in such a vulnerable position again.'

Josh nodded. He knew the risks and his eyes swiftly scanned the rest of the slope with some measure of trepidation. 'Once that boulder begins to move, it won't just bring our guards down, more like the whole hillside, burying the gold for ever. Us too, if we're not careful.'

'If you don't, we'll never see a cent's worth of this

gold or any other,' returned Jim *sotto voce.* He signalled for Billy to haul away on the hoist, drawing up the first two bars. 'If I know Gilt Bartram, he's relaxing down by the wagons. Riddick Tomms is on close guard duties – he'll accompany Sera and Billy down the slopes with the gold bars. If we allow him a minute or two to get clear before we pull the plug, that'll give us time to climb out of this rat hole. First off, I'll knock out some of the supports in the cave to give the guards something to take their minds off you. Soon as the cave collapses, you haul away.'

'What happens then?'

'With any luck we'll pick up at least one of the guards' rifles. Bartram and Tomms will be on their way up here, hotfoot, so just as soon as we're out of the canyon, you'll have to provide some sort of diversion, anything to take their eyes off me. I don't doubt they'll secure Sera and Billy before they leave the wagons, but if I can make it down there and release them, we'll have numbers on our side.'

Josh shook his massive head. 'It's dangerous,' he warned. 'That ridge the guards are standing on extends over the mouth of the cave. You'll be buried under the debris with the gold if you don't look lively.'

'Never mind me. Can you do it?' Jim's face was as serious as the big ex-sergeant had ever seen it.

'Like you say, it's our only chance,' he agreed. He

118

spat on his hands in a workmanlike manner.

Jim nodded and smiled encouragingly. He dropped to his knees and began to worm his way back into the narrow cavern; then he stretched full length on his belly to grasp the furthest support. He had no intention of being trapped by the collapsing roof, and he curled himself into position to make a rapid exit.

Patience was a virtue he'd cultivated during long hours playing cards for high stakes, but the stakes he played for now were higher still, and he had to take a firm grip on his nerves, carefully counting out the time his companions would take to reach the wagons. The further off Riddick Tomms and his deadly guns were, the longer they'd have to pull off their stunt.

Now, he told himself, and hauled on the support. The rocks above had settled and jammed the wood hard in, but the gambler held the strength of desperation in the cracking muscles of his extended arms. The support gave and the roof began to move. Jim shot out of the hole like a startled rabbit, followed by a low rumbling crash and an explosion of dust and splintered rock.

He stared up and signalled to the startled guards above. They both had their eyes fixed on the smoking entrance to the gold cavern and not on their other captive. He was stripped to the waist and

Jim could see the banded cords of muscle swelling on his massive body while he toiled at his task. No ordinary man could have moved that rock, but, despite his age, Josh O'Donnel was a veritable Samson and even as Jim watched a crack opened up under the guards' feet.

'Damn you.' One of the guards at last spotted the danger, but before he could do more than raise his rifle, the ledge collapsed under him and he was thrown off his feet.

A louder rumble followed the first, signalling a far worse avalanche. Bereft of the rocks below, the entire, unstable hillside began to crumble away. The second guard, horror etched into his face, disappeared into the maw of a suddenly opened chasm at his feet, then the whole disappeared into a mêlée of thunderous noise and crumbling rock, the dust raising a curtain over a scene from hell.

Appalled by the destruction he'd started, Jim sprinted to the far corner of the canyon's narrow expanse, barely aware that Josh was hot on his heels. The slithering rock face seemed to leap across the void towards them and Jim flung himself on to the sheer cliff, scrabbling desperately to haul himself up the few feet necessary to survive.

Then, as quickly as it had started, the noise subsided and the dust swirled upwards to reveal a vista of devastation to the startled gambler. Josh lay a few feet to his right, straining to lift the jagged weight of a boulder that pinned his leg. Jim shoved his shoulder under it and heaved until it shifted far enough for the big man to free himself.

'Get moving,' he called, unnerved by the sudden silence that had settled over the scene. 'No chance of finding a gun down here.'

That much was obvious to the gambler; the guards had disappeared as completely as though they'd never been there, but the rock fall, unstable though it was, had at least simplified the climb out of the boxed-in canyon. The rim was no longer as high as once it had been, and neither were the slopes so steep. Desperate to reach his goal before either of his enemies could cut off his escape, Jim risked everything in his frantic bid for freedom. Only when he reached the top did he turn to see whether Josh had followed him.

He had, though not quite so quickly, and Jim breathed a sigh of relief. He'd been worried the big man might have taken an injury, curtailing any attempt at scaling the cliff. He searched down the slopes towards the wagons too, but with a ragged curtain of dust obliterating the slopes, he could see no sign of either Gilt Bartram or Riddick Tomms.

Taken by surprise by the avalanche, they'd take the direct route up, he decided. He elected to attempt the steeper slopes on their flank. Too steep for care, as he was well aware, and his feet soon slithered out from beneath him in the slippery scree. A crumpling crash into a larger rock knocked the breath out of his lungs, but he'd regained control of his descent and, ignoring the pain, he swung himself from hold to precarious hold. Another slide, but he was already nearly at the foot of the cliff and came to no harm.

A shell whined off the rocks and Jim realized he'd been spotted, but only from far above. He sprinted again, the blood thundering through his veins while he fought for his breath. Had they fired at him again? He didn't know, but at length he was sheltered by the wagons. Their guns were still piled in its well, and he picked a rifle at random, levering shells into its barrel and firing indiscriminately at the hillside while he searched around for his companions.

Sera was pinioned to one of the big wheels and, having retrieved his knife, the gambler quickly cut her free and hauled her into the shelter of the wagon.

'Where are they?' he breathed into her ear. 'I lost sight of them.'

The sound of horses galloping off answered his question, but by the time Jim had broken cover, no one was in sight.

Josh arrived at a lumbering run, favouring his left leg, which bled copiously from an open wound, presumably a souvenir of the rock which pinned him down in the canyon.

'They've taken the horses,' he pointed out, nodding towards their makeshift corral which no longer held any of their animals.

'Scattered them more like,' replied Jim, serene now that the worst was past, 'but the draught horses won't stray far.' He pointed out across the wilderness where he could already see a couple of them standing around looking lost. 'Let them get the smell of water in their nostrils and they'll come back of their own accord.'

'What do we do about Billy?' Sera asked the question, but the little man's fate was on all their minds. 'I don't trust him further than I can throw him.'

'I'd like to crush his scrawny neck,' Josh agreed vindictively, 'but I guess I'll settle on leaving him to the desert.'

'We may need his help in fighting off the Comancheros,' Jim reminded them both. 'Bartram may have ridden off, but only to fetch help. He isn't the sort to give up when there's gold for the taking.'

'We can't trust the little weasel with a gun.'

'No,' the gambler agreed, 'but Bartram is his enemy as much as ours.' He took the fateful decision. 'Soon as we can get enough horses rounded up, we'll set off in the wagon. Billy can remain trussed up until the outlaws are on our trail. Time enough to arm him then.'

'What about the gold?'

'It'd take an army to dig that up now, Josh. We've already packed enough to make us all rich, but Gilt Bartram will take that if he catches us.'

'He's bound to. The wagon's too slow in this terrain – any terrain come to that. He'll be on us within an hour or two.'

'I hope not,' replied Jim confidently. 'He told me himself that his gang's been dispatched on a raid to keep them occupied. He needed them out of the way while he made his own escape, and that will count in our favour too.'

Josh laughed, genuine humour in his eyes for once. 'Hoist by his own petard,' he exclaimed.

'Not quite,' the gambler reminded him. 'Bartram has an edge denied to us. He knows where he sent his men. I'll lay you long odds he'll be on our tail within twenty-four hours.' Having delivered this bombshell he went on: 'We'll head for the fort at Whitney. It lies considerably further off than Madison, but if they attempt to cut us off rather than follow our trail, it may cost them a few more hours on the chase. They won't want to approach the military too closely either.'

'I'll round up the horses,' agreed Josh. 'One of them's already ambling in.' He strode out to meet the animal with a handful of fresh feed.

'Looks like you saved the day.' Sera leaned up

124

close to Jim Murphy and ran her hand up his arm.

'Not me,' he declined. 'Josh is the one who pulled the rug out from under them.'

'Then perhaps this belongs to him.' Sera twined her arms around the gambler's neck and gently laid her cool, soft lips on his own.

Jim could have agreed, but he didn't. One long arm snaked about her waist, chaining her to his length, while the other forked through the thick mass of her hair. She subsided into him, kissing harder, deeper, opening her mouth under his own, while the soft weight of her breasts lay crushed against his chest. He felt his instinctive reaction to her scent, the raw need for her lithe body, the way she switched her hips against his burgeoning loins.

'Now ain't that nice,' a familiar voice cut into their union.

CHAPTER TWELVE

THE GUNMAN WITHIN

Sera stepped back with a startled gasp. Both Jim and she swivelled their eyes towards the front of the wagon.

Black Riddick Tomms stood there, laughing at their evident surprise. 'You didn't suppose I'd just go away and leave you without saying goodbye?' he mocked. 'That wouldn't be polite.'

Jim, suddenly aware of the way Tomms's right hand was hovering over his pistol, fanned away from the wagon and Sera. The gunman was evidently going to offer him a chance to outdraw him.

'Zack Holmes told me you were mighty quick on the draw.' Riddick Tomms confirmed the gambler's thoughts. 'Said you'd pulled your gun on a drummer in New Orleans and he barely saw you move.' He sniggered expectantly. 'Reckon most folks can beat a salesman to the draw, but I ain't selling nothing, less'n it's your death warrant.'

Tomms was over-confident, Jim decided; he was trying to prod him into drawing first. He edged further away from Sera while his brain worked overtime. Perhaps the gunman had reason for his confidence. Gentleman Jim Murphy had something of a reputation up and down the river, but the name of Black Riddick Tomms was feared far and wide. He was pure poison on the draw, greased lightning, and a cold-eyed killer to boot, but none of these fears showed in the gambler's face. The gambler hadn't practised poker with the best players on the river only to let his opponent read his sombre thoughts.

'Cat got your tongue?' Riddick Tomms tried again, and once again Jim ignored him while he sought a way out of the puzzle.

Sera hadn't retrieved her weapon yet. Pray God she wouldn't try and force the gunman into turning his guns on her. Had Josh picked up a gun before he left to round up the horses? He must have, but he'd be too far off to interfere in this fight; perhaps he'd be able to save the girl.

The seconds were stretching out, feeling more like minutes to his overwrought nerves, and Jim could feel his tongue lying dry in his mouth. The metallic taste of fear was etched into his throat, but he could see too, that his opponent felt the same sensations. Riddick Tomms wasn't as confident as he tried to make out. He too was vulnerable, all the more so for his overweaning conceit that no one could face his fast draw and live. There was always another one who was faster, and Jim decided there and then that, even if he wasn't fast enough, at least he'd be strong enough to get his shot off before he died.

His mind turned icily clear and he prepared to do battle. Riddick Tomms was only a man, he told himself. Sure, he was a gunman, fast on the draw, but not as fast as Gentleman Jim Murphy. A lie, as he already suspected, but it was one he could tell himself with a clear conscience.

Sera, shaken by the developing stand-off, suddenly snaked her hand over the side of the wagon, seeking a weapon, any weapon. Riddick Tomms spotted the move and allowed himself to be diverted. No more than a moment, but that was all Jim Murphy needed. Gilt Bartram had told the truth; Jim's draw was mighty quick, but not fast enough to beat the speed of Black Riddick Tomms. The gunman's distraction had been momentary, his hands mesmerizingly quick, a sure-fired blur of sheer adrenaline, the pistol leaping into his fist as if of its own accord.

The diversion had told, however. Tomms still fired

a split second before the gambler, but his aim was wide, the result of attempting to divide his attention between two targets. Jim's aim remained sure, despite the buzz of a bullet whistling close by his ear, the wind of its passage seeming to ruffle his hair.

The dynamics of the fight changed with immediate effect. Black Riddick Tomms had been badly hit, but it wasn't a fatal wound and he dived under the wheels of the wagon, rolling over and over to disturb his opponent's aim. Sera vaulted athletically into the well of the wagon and disappeared from view, while Jim hit the floor and opened up on the gunman's frantically jinking body. The man might have been hard hit, but he was still lively enough to inflict serious damage if the gambler couldn't finish him.

Tomms broke free of the wagon and sprinted towards the cover of the nearby rock fall, a bloody wound in his chest still pumping blood. Sera stood on the wagon's prow and levered shell after shell after him, while even Josh managed to get in on the act, firing on the gunman from long range whilst attempting to rein in a posse of nervous horses. Just who, in the end, shot Black Riddick Tomms down remained a mystery that none of them sought to solve; but it wasn't Gentleman Jim Murphy – his pistol had already exhausted its full complement of bullets.

*

'Where's Billy?' Josh O'Donnel asked the question as soon as he'd chivvied in his haul of horseflesh, more than enough to transport their one good wagon across the desert.

Jim scooted around the wagon; the treacherous little weasel had been safely roped on to the far wheel when he'd last looked, but evidently Gilt Bartram and Riddick Tomms hadn't paid enough attention to his bonds. Billy Harkness had freed himself and gone to ground.

'Just as well,' Josh put all their thoughts into words. 'Saves me finding an excuse to wring his scrawny neck.'

'Get the horses put to,' Jim decided, rapidly reloading his pistol, 'while I scout around. If Billy sees us leaving, he may open up on us. Last thing we need is casualties, when the Holmes gang is on our tail.'

He stepped out into the open and surveyed the nearby cliffs, carefully searching for anything out of the ordinary, the flash of a reflection from the sun on a gun barrel for instance. There was plenty of cover, enough for the man to hide from an army, but the gambler had an uneasy feeling that Billy was doing no such thing. He scouted around the big prairie wagon, peering into the well of the lopsided vehicle, still sitting awry without the axle they'd removed to provide their cover story for the tell-tale forge.

Josh and Sera had ceased their careless chatter, but Jim Murphy realized it a little too late.

A roar of rage suddenly broke the brief silence. Josh's angry challenge was evidently intended for Billy Harkness's benefit, but it was cut off as quickly as it was made by the sharp explosion of a pistol. Sera screamed and Jim broke away from the immobilized prairie wagon.

Billy was waiting for him. He had the girl's throat locked in the crook of his arm, held in front of him as a protective shield. Her face was pale, shocked by the sudden violence.

'Stay where you are, Jim,' Billy Harkness called out, holding his pistol to Sera's head.

'Don't be a fool.' Jim steadied his headlong rush, but nevertheless continued to advance slowly towards the pair. Josh was lying still and silent on the ground, a few paces to their rear, dead or unconscious. Without a closer examination of the body, it was impossible for the gambler to decide which.

'Drop the gun.' Billy tightened his grip on Sera, his forearm cutting cruelly into her windpipe. The girl began to gag, her hands wrenching on the other's arm, but without any visible result. 'She's dead meat,' warned Billy, 'unless you do just what I say.'

'Let her go, Billy.' Jim began to back off, holding his pistol loosely to one side. 'You won't get far on your own.'

'Far as I want to go,' the treacherous little weasel returned. He cocked the pistol and ground the barrel hard into the side of the girl's head, making her wince. 'I'm getting mighty tired of waiting for you. Drop it now, or I'll blow her head off.'

Jim could see murder in the little man's eyes. He judged the odds and threw his pistol to the ground, far enough to appease his opponent, but not so far that he couldn't make a dive for it if the situation altered. Billy was far too cagey to allow him a clear shot at his head, and doing nothing was about as smart as making a shot that would only wound the man. Either way the girl would die, and as Jim had belatedly realized, he couldn't bear that to happen.

'Let her go,' he called out.

'Not likely,' Billy crowed, suddenly aware he'd won. 'She's my ticket out of here.' He wrenched the slight figure of his captive around and flung her headlong on to the wagon, before lightly springing up himself. Josh had evidently completed putting the horses to and Billy whipped them into a gallop as soon as he'd taken the reins.

'Goodbye, Jim,' he waved cheerily, then took careful aim at the gambler.

It was a long shot at such a range on a rumbling wagon, and predictably the flying bullets went nowhere near their intended target, or maybe Billy was just seeking to dissuade the gambler from

132

coming after him.

'Josh.' Having retrieved his pistol, Jim knelt by the side of his fallen companion. He'd seen death before, and it didn't need the search for a pulse to confirm his diagnosis. He turned the still body and saw the scarlet blood. Josh had been shot through the heart.

Jim sighed and stared out across the desert towards the distant wagon. The vehicle itself had disappeared behind one of the crumbing, rocky spires that dominated the landscape, but its path was still marked by a plume of smokelike dust.

'You're a dead man, Billy,' he promised.

CHAPTER THIRTEEN

TREACHERY REPAID

Jim Murphy took the time to bury his companion properly, even down to saying a few words over the grave. It was a long time since he'd done that, and it showed how far their brief companionship had advanced. That done, he looked up with a grimace; the sun was high in the sky and he was low on water.

Fortunately Josh had splashed some of the precious liquid into their makeshift trough for the horses. Jim used what remained to fill his water bottle, shaking his head over how little he had. Josh had carried a bottle on his person, and Jim had taken that too, but it all added up to very little for trekking in the desert, even though he intended to travel only in the cool of the night.

Tracing the heavy wagon wouldn't test his abilities as a tracker, even under the palest of moonlight, but he wouldn't catch up with Billy. Not until he'd reached civilization at any rate, though the treacherous little toad would have to stop somewhere, if only to recover the gold from its hiding-place. Selling the precious metal in bulk would inevitably draw him to a city, and it was there that Jim Murphy would hunt him down.

Sera? What would Billy do with her? Jim settled himself down in a hollow under a boulder close by the cliffs, seeking shade from the flaming heat of the afternoon sun while he thought on the problem. It was the girl he was really chasing, not the gold. He came to that conclusion with very little consideration. If he had to relinquish the gold to save her, then he'd do so without a qualm.

A thunder of hoofs caught at his ears and he peered anxiously out of his shadowed concealment. A bunch of heavily armed Comancheros was storming across the desert sands towards the deserted prairie wagon, Gilt Bartram, or was it Holmes, at their head? So much for their hopes of gaining a lead on the cunning outlaw leader; his gang must have been lying close enough for him to round them up almost instantly.

Jim studied them while they surrounded the

disabled wagon, a couple dismounting to poke inside its capacious well. Gilt Bartram edged his horse across to the freshly dug grave and stared down at it reflectively. He raised his eyes to survey the nearby cliff face, but, evidently finding nothing to keep him, began to follow the clear track of Billy's wagon, calling in his men behind him.

Jim watched until they too disappeared from sight, then set off in their wake at a loping run. They'd run Billy down in the next few hours, by his reckoning. It'd be dark, and most likely they'd make camp and celebrate their success; the wagon's capacious well was still full of liquor – and then there was Sera. His face took on a rigid expression of unrelenting enmity when he thought of what they might do to the girl once she was in their hands.

He heard the gunshots from far off, but he didn't relax his pace though the sweat poured off him. Despite having very little water, he used it unsparingly, knowing he couldn't continue at his present pace without it. Billy, and most probably by the time he came up on them, the outlaws too, had water; several full barrels still lay in the wagon's well. The four companions had deliberately kept the life-giving liquid in their one serviceable wagon in case they should be forced to make a run for it themselves.

The distant shots ceased of a sudden and Jim

mentally consigned Billy to the devil, for hell was exactly where the treacherous little killer would end up. They'd keep Sera to amuse them, for a while at least, so long as she too hadn't stopped a bullet in the exchange of fire.

Jim eventually came upon the outlaws' camp a couple of hours after nightfall. He'd seen the reflection of their fires way off and had slackened his pace to creep up on them unawares. A noble sentiment, but quite unnecessary, it appeared. So far as he could see the Comancheros kept no guard, though they'd pulled the wagon up in the lee of a hillside almost as rocky as the ridge they'd just left.

He crept closer, trying to see what was going on. Somehow he'd expected them to be busily recovering the gold, but none of them seemed to be interested in crawling underneath the wagon to get at the precious metal. Instead they were staring hungrily at the canvas covering from which Sera was slowly emerging. Evidently Gilt Bartram had kept the valuable secret from them. His eyes widened when he took in the girl's skimpy dress.

Sera was evidently slated to perform for the Comanchero gang, but it was to be no ordinary performance, that much was plain. The drunken band were evidently auctioning her favours, shouting out their offers to an amused-looking Gilt Bartram, while she shivered miserably, exposed for their benefit in a costume deliberately designed to inflate their interest and their bids.

Jim watched for a while, his face hard, while Sera's shrinking form was thrust forward for the crowd's delectation, dressed in no more than a brief camisole, unlaced across its front, and a torn petticoat that showed off one leg to the top of her thigh. His own angry growl was drowned by a cacophony of catcalls and jeers from the inebriated crowd gathered around the wagon, still calling out their bids while she began to sing for them. Slowly he withdrew, to work his way further around their camp.

Sera was well into her second song by the time he reached his intended target, the bow of the wagon, and the furthest point from the group of outlaws crowded around the makeshift stage at its rear. He slid silently under the canvas top, though with the way they were shouting and cheering he could have made whatever noise he chose. Since the girl's performance was understandably muted, the gambler could only presume the applause was meant to celebrate her lewdly displayed figure.

'Hold their attention,' he hissed once she'd finished her number, uncomfortably aware that, though the canvas was thick, Gilt Bartram was also standing too close by for comfort. 'Soon as I open up, dive back under here.' He'd had to keep his voice to a whisper, but Sera immediately made it apparent she'd understood him by picking up her performance. The next song was more upbeat and all her former listlessness disappeared when she swung into the number, parading up and down the makeshift stage while she brandished her petticoat, flicking it up to show off her shapely legs and draw whoops of delight from the assembled men.

'Make her strip,' someone called from the audience and she reacted to a fresh chorus of appreciation by peeling the camisole top down her own shoulders, teasing them with the cleavage she'd revealed. The bids redoubled in a burst of fresh enthusiasm and she danced on as though she welcomed their attentions, artfully driving the outlaw crowd into a frenzy that was due to be ended as quickly and shockingly as it started.

Jim had been willing to face down the vicious gang of outlaws with only his pistol to back him up, but thankfully he discovered their own rifles still stored in the capacious well. He laid two easily to hand and filled his pockets with additional shells before laying out Sera's standard working clothes. Her freshly invigorated performance gave him time to prepare and he took it, peering through a tear in the canvas screen to mark down his targets. Gilt Bartram was one, but perhaps the clever outlaw chief had already been alerted by Sera's resurgent display, or he was merely tired of the game, for the cunning killer was nowhere to be seen.

This was no time for procrastination and Jim seized his moment, opening up a positive barrage from the first of his rifles. The startled outlaws were taken by complete surprise, and it wasn't until several had already gone down under the sudden hail of lead that they began to scatter, hauling out their own guns to retaliate. Sera too, had been shocked by the sudden onslaught, quite unprepared for the wholesale slaughter that was unleashed, but she was at least forewarned and, quickly recovering her wits, she dived through the canvas to join her rescuer.

'Out,' he ordered peremptorily. 'Grab those clothes and make for the rocks.' He dropped the first rifle and took up a second, barely wasting a glance on the girl before he opened up again.

Some of the Comanchero band were firing back by now, but with only their handguns within easy reach, no cover to rely on and all of them rapidly retreating from his assault, their overwhelming superiority in numbers wasn't able to make itself felt as yet.

Neither would it if the gambler could help it. Not immediately, at any rate. Jim emptied the rifle and followed the girl over the side of the wagon, escaping easily into the dark. Tomorrow might tell a different story, but they'd be safe for the night. No one in the outlaw gang would be anxious to track down a killer in the dark, even with the light of the moon to guide them, more especially since they'd no means of knowing just how many men had been involved in the attack. Jim had fired into the assembled mass as fast as he could pull the trigger, not bothering to pick and choose his targets, and could easily have been mistaken for two or even three avenging gunmen.

Gilt Bartram wouldn't have been fooled though, and Jim feared his leadership more than the entire pack of Comancheros. Where was he? Evidently he'd chosen to keep the secret of the gold to himself, but what good would it do him now that the wagon was in outlaw hands? None at all, unless he could ensure the two fugitives were killed, and so were no longer able to divulge the secrets he preferred to leave concealed. No doubt the outlaw chief would be organizing his men ready for an attack at dawn, and with several of their comrades wounded or even dead, they'd be in no mood for compromise.

Jim raced into the cover of a group of boulders littered under the main part of the rocky cliff which backed outlaws' campsite, still considering what their optionsmight be. Under the scant light provided by the moon Sera's pale form was momentarily revealed, struggling in the grip of one of the outlaws, whose wits had evidently been quicker than the rest. The gambler cannoned into him, whirling the stock of his empty rifle to knock him off balance.

The faceless Comanchero came at him immediately, before he had any chance to go for his pistol. The moonlight reflected eerily on the knife in his hands and Jim swung his gun again, this time using the barrel to strike back at his opponent. The man was too fast, however, and, avoiding the attempt to stun him, ran forward weaving his knife in a mesmerizing arc of flashing steel. The slash was aimed at his throat, but Jim deflected the lethal thrust with an adroit twist of his rifle and retaliated by slamming the stock directly into his opponent's face.

The outlaw gave ground, but showed no sign of surrendering. With that deadly knife within inches of him the gambler dare not drop the empty rifle, his only means of blocking his opponent's attacks, to try for his pistol. In the end it was Sera who broke the deadlock. She'd been watching the fight with wide, frightened eyes, unable to offer help, but when the outlaw eventually leapt back from one of the gambler's more vicious strikes, she thrust out her foot.

The man fell backwards, dropping his knife, but clawing for his pistol. Jim's own draw was too fast for him however; the gambler fired before his own rifle had hit the ground. Jim swiftly bent over the man's body, feeling for signs of life.

142

'Is he dead?' Sera asked the question.

'He is.' Jim looked up at the girl who seemed unconcerned by the carnage around her while she slipped out of her camisole and prepared to pull on the shirt. She acknowledged his glance with a half-hearted grin, but made no self-conscious attempts to hide her bare breasts from him. Neither did she balk at tearing off the ragged remains of her petticoat to replace it with the thick work-trousers he'd picked out for her. Not that her modesty suffered unduly, Jim had already turned away to study their opponents' dispositions.

Most of the outlaws, as he could clearly see, were gathered behind the wagon, though a few were scattered haphazardly across the desert floor, taking cover behind whatever rock or fold in the ground would hide them. Jim noted with grim satisfaction that their own position was naturally fortified against attack. The cliff behind was steep enough to discourage any attempt to encircle them, and the desert in front was a perfect killing ground, clear of anything that might hide their enemies if they attempted a hazardous frontal attack. Nevertheless it was clear that Bartram had organized his men very quickly following the sudden onslaught that had caught them all by surprise. No wonder his bloody reign as Zachariah Holmes had proved so successful.

What now? Would he consider a night attack? Or

would he starve them out? Jim had no more than a part-filled water bottle, and even with strict rationing, it wouldn't be long before the desert did its work for the Comanchero's chief. They might last another twenty-four hours if they didn't stop a bullet, but the following day would inevitably see the merciless glare of the sun suck the last vestiges of moisture from their lifeless carcasses.

Sera slid into position close beside him, her shapely form pressed hard against his own muscled length. She too held a rifle, and Jim could only admire her courage and foresight in thinking to gather up the gun while her own position was still so uncertain.

'I'm beholden,' he admitted.

'Me too,' she confirmed with a nod as she slid her weapon forward. 'My rifle's empty, though.'

More than beholden, she confessed to herself while she watched him slip a clutch of shells from his pockets. This was one man she could give herself to without fear he'd leave her in the lurch.

CHAPTER FOURTEEN

ESCAPE AT HAND

'What's happening now?' Sera stared out across the wide panorama, calmly picking out the waiting Comancheros' positions while she spoke. 'Are they going to launch an attack?'

'They won't do anything until dawn,' Jim answered confidently, though in truth he was still unsure whether or not Gilt Bartram might drive his men forward in an attack by moonlight. It didn't seem likely, for the ghostly light was bright enough to illuminate the open ground, while they still lay hidden in the shadows. As Bartram would be able to judge for himself, any such assault would be suicidal, but then again, the outlaw chief probably didn't care how many men he lost. Nevertheless, waiting until daylight would at least enable his men to see their enemy and realize how much easier a war of attrition would be.

'They're moving the wagon.'

Jim switched his attention on to the moonlit camp. The girl was right, the wagon was being hitched up.

'Bartram,' he breathed. 'He's going to make a run for it, leaving his men here to finish us off.'

'He can't do that.'

'He's just done it.' Jim watched the wagon pull away from the campsite, a dozen outlaws scattering out across the desert floor when their cover deserted them. 'On his own, too.'

'We can't let him get away with it.' Sera's voice mirrored her desperation. All their hard work was fast slipping through their fingers.

'We'll be lucky to escape with our own lives,' Jim warned her grimly, 'but Bartram may have made a mistake for once in his life.'

'What. . . ?'

'He'll turn east, soon as he's out of sight,' predicted the gambler. 'He daren't risk heading for a fort, too much chance he'd be recognized as Zachariah Holmes and hanged. Madison is a much safer haven for a wanted man like him. He knows people there, can probably even pause to recover the gold from its hiding lace and take his place as Gilt Bartram. Once he's regained his credits as a

Southern gentleman, he'll be welcomed wherever he goes, especially if he has cash in his pockets.'

'I still don't see. . . .'

'East is that way.' Jim jerked his head towards the cliff behind them. 'He'll have to circumnavigate this entire hillside to get back on track. If we can cross it direct, we may be able to cut him off.' He stared at the setting moon. 'It'll be even darker when the moon sets, and we'll be able to climb out of here unseen.' He made the rough calculation in his head and frowned. 'We'll have a couple of hours to complete the ascent before sunrise.'

'It's impossible.' Sera had scanned the cliff too. 'It's much too steep for us to climb.'

'We'll have to dump the rifles and find any handholds we can,' the gambler replied, mentally planning his route up the treacherous rock. 'The first twenty feet is the worst, the sand has scoured it clean. After that it's up to us.'

'Can we really do it?' Sera remained unconvinced, but she already knew the alternative was impossible. Staying where they were was a one-way ticket to the graveyard.

'Depends on how wide the hills behind these cliffs are. If we miss Bartram then we'll be stuck in the middle of the desert with no water.' He held up his bottle and sloshed the remaining contents around to reinforce his point.

*

'Time to go,' Jim whispered at last. The moon had disappeared behind the horizon as suddenly as it had appeared.

'Good luck.' For a moment Sera clung on to the gambler, kissing him hard on the lips.

'You too,' he returned, his voice echoing the slightly shaken feel in his legs. Her unexpected embrace had caught him on the hop.

Climbing a vertical cliff by feel soon concentrated his mind. Jim had already marked down a barely visible crack that led them up the first twenty feet, but after that they'd be dependent on a fine sense of touch to find the handholds. He pushed back his fears and began to work his way up the line of the fault, clinging on with his fingertips while his boots scrambled to find enough purchase to hold him on the cliff. It was too dark to see the girl, but he could hear her. Sera's breath hissed through her teeth while she followed his lead.

One hand reached the far point of the crack he'd been following and he paused until the girl caught him up and he could point out their next move.

'It's a leap of faith,' he told her grimly. 'There's a narrow ledge off to my right, just close enough to get a handhold on it.' He tried to sound more confident. 'It's too big to miss.'

Or at least it looked that way from below, he decided. When he was twenty feet up a vertical cliff and facing a leap in the dark towards a ledge he couldn't even see, it didn't seem quite so large. He stiffened his nerves: waiting wouldn't bring it any closer, and made a crablike side leap. His fingertips clutched wildly at thin air, and for a moment, he thought he'd misjudged. His heart leapt into his mouth. He was falling; and then, all of a sudden, one hand was touching the ledge and he was swinging loose. His fingers began to slip under his own weight, and he hooked them into claws, as though to dig them into solid rock. The slide ceased and a moment later he was hauling himself up by main force, his laboured breathing disguising just how shaken he was.

From his new position on the relative safety of the ledge, which was wider than he'd ever suspected, he could easily see Sera's trim figure outlined against the lighter background of the sky. He knelt down on one knee and reached out his hand towards her.

'Jump,' he murmured quietly, all too aware that a parcel of outlaws was still within easy pistol range of their exposed position on the hillside.

Sera did so, aiming for the sound of his voice. A real leap of faith, considering she hadn't even seen the ledge. Jim caught hold of her wrists and hauled her on to the narrow ledge.

149

'It's easy from here,' he assured her confidently, breathing in her scent while he held her close and whispered in her ear.

Easy it might have been after the rigours of the initial ascent, but not so comfortable that they could afford to relax. The slope was no longer vertical, but it was still steep enough to challenge both their balance and their nerve. It was still too dark to spot their holds, but using a sense of touch they were able to make good progress up the cliff. The sun shone on them before it hit the outlaw camp below, but by that time they'd discovered a narrow fissure that led them off the main cliff face and deep into the rocky interior.

Dark chasms still opened up under their feet with unnerving regularity, but once the first rays of the dawn began to illuminate their progress, they began to move faster. At the high point of their climb, a windswept, exposed ridge of treacherously friable rock, Jim called a short halt, doling out a small measure of their valuable water, before examining the way forward.

'There's sand ahead,' he told Sera, who'd dropped to her knees from sheer exhaustion. 'With any luck that's the trail Bartram will take to Madison.'

'Let's go then.' She dragged herself wearily to her feet and began to pick her way through the rock-strewn hills on the gambler's heels.

'There he is.' Jim was in the lead and spotted Bartram a second or two before the girl. He was too far off for them to hear the rattle of his progress yet, but then they were far off their own objective too, a couple of hundred feet above the sandy floor that marked the outlaw chief's route, on as sheer a cliff as she'd ever seen.

'He's got to pass through that chasm ahead.' Sera had marked it out, but, for the life of her, couldn't see how they'd reach it in time.

'Perfect spot for an ambush,' Jim agreed. He began to leap from rock to rock, following the edge of the cliff and constantly searching for the way down.

'Here,' he told Sera at last. There'd been a rock fall at some time in the none too distant past and the jagged boulders still lay piled up against the cliffs. A patch of loose scree ran along a jagged fissure some eight to ten feet below them and led directly on to the fall.

Jim Murphy regarded it with some trepidation. The cliff was sheer beneath his feet and they'd have to jump on to the narrow band of loose dust and stone. It would almost certainly shift under their weight, but in which direction? If it spilled out over the edge of the cliff they were doomed!

Gilt Bartram suddenly swung into sight almost immediately below them and Jim took his chance. If they couldn't stop the outlaw chief they'd be dead of thirst by the end of the day. He'd take a chance of going over the cliff, and so would the girl. The gambler grasped her hand and they leapt over the cliff edge together.

They landed amongst the scree, their heels digging into the loose material, but they'd kept their feet. A spurt of loose rock and dust careered off the edge of the fissure, but they were caught in the main stream of the sudden avalanche, riding a wave of detritus down towards the rock fall. Dust and stones seemed to erupt into the air alongside them, and inevitably they fell, a maelstrom of noise and dust settling around them.

'Come on.' Jim sensed they'd escaped the worst and made a dive for a solitary boulder that seemed to be held fast by its own massive weight. Sera careered on past, the slope still moving under her feet, and disappeared into a huge mushroom of dust and detritus that erupted when the moving scree hit the main rock fall with a drawn-out roar. The ground began to shake beneath the gambler's feet, and for a moment he wondered if they'd caused the entire hillside to crumble. Then, of a sudden, the earth stopped moving and he could scramble on.

The slope was easier here, despite the blinding dust that cut down visibility to no more than a few yards. Thrusting Sera's fate to the back of his mind,

Jim took his life into his hands and leapt spring-heeled from boulder to boulder until he reached flat sand. Gilt Bartram had to be stopped and he ran forward into the dust laden gloom, hauling out his pistol. The outlaw would be desperate and in no mood to surrender lightly.

He emerged into the sunlight at a run. The wagon was no more than a few feet distant, and its driver as surprised by the gambler's sudden appearance as Jim Murphy was to see his enemy so close.

Jim fired first, in no mood to offer quarter, but Bartram's quick wits saved his life as surely as they surrendered the wagon. He knew Jim was the better man in a fire-fight; he dived off the driving seat, hitting the ground at a run. A second shot sped him on his way as he disappeared into the rapidly settling dust cloud with the gambler in hot pursuit. The game was to be played out amongst the treacherous boulder-strewn slopes of the rock fall.

If it hadn't been for Sera, Jim would have given up there and then. He had the wagon and Gilt Bartram was welcome to all the desert he could find. Without water the outlaw was as helpless as they'd been so short a time before, but the girl could still be alive, probably was, and Jim knew he couldn't leave her for all the gold in the world. Neither could he afford to take any risks and let Bartram off the hook; if he died and Bartram escaped, then Sera's fate was sealed too.

He settled himself in good cover and waited for the dust to die away. Once he could see his quarry, he'd take him. Take him for all the good men who'd died at his whim.

Sera was the difference. She'd seen the wagon, heard the shots and, higher up the slopes, she could see Bartram too.

'Watch your back,' she called out, breaking cover to warn the gambler that Gilt Bartram was creeping up on him. She dropped back, quick as a jack rabbit, when the outlaw snapped off a shot at her.

Jim had last seen Bartram on the run, and hadn't yet realized that the hunt was a two-way thing. He cursed himself for a fool and crept forward with increased vigilance, climbing into the jumble of rocks and boulders on a mission of vengeance that would end only when he'd killed his man.

Wrong again!

Once more it was Sera who'd seen the danger first. 'Riders,' she called out from her high eyrie and beckoned to Jim to join her. 'It's the Holmes gang.'

Jim Murphy cursed under his breath again and made haste to reunite himself with his companion. They'd come so far, only to fall into the same old trap, holed up under the guns of the outlaw band.

Gilt Bartram scuttled out from behind a boulder on the edge of the rock fall and ran towards his rapidly approaching men. A fusillade of shots rang out and he fell.

'They've killed him.' Sera turned to Jim as he arrived by her side, and flung herself into his arms, hardly able to believe her eyes.

'Rumbled him, more like,' the gambler told her. 'Discovered he was about to double-cross them and run off with the gold.' He folded his arms about her and drew her down. 'They may take the wagon and leave us alone.' It was a forlorn hope and he knew it. The rocky slope could cover the approach of an army, and they'd be as mad as a disturbed hornets' nest at his part in freeing Sera.

CHAPTER FIFTEEN

AT THE END OF THE DAY

Battle was quickly joined. Even before the Comncheros melted into the boulder-strewn slope they were firing ragged volleys at Jim and Sera, forcing them to keep their heads down. The gambler was constrained, moreover, to limit his own return fire. Ironically, although he had a pocket full of rifle shells, he only had a pistol to defend himself with, and the girl, nothing at all.

He'd take as many of them with him as he could and then turn the gun upon Sera and himself at the last, he decided.

The firing redoubled and he popped up his head.

They wouldn't be wasting so much lead unless the final assault was due to begin. Damned bad shots too: the bullets were nowhere near him. He stared out amazed when another group of riders tore in from the desert, a lone bugler sounding the charge. Dark uniforms, dusty and stained from days on the trail, but still recognizably blue. The cavalry had arrived.

The outlaws scattered, taking to their horses and, adroitly avoiding the military column, disappeared into the desert wastes they knew so well.

'You were lucky, mister.' The major in charge of the column faced Jim and Sera, taking in their torn, stained clothing. 'We heard the shots from way off and took the chance to interfere.'

'Murphy,' the gambler offered. 'Jim Murphy, and this here's Sera.' He held out a filthy hand which the officer shook with evident distaste. 'We're glad to see you, Major.'

'I'll bet.' The major could see they'd been fighting the outlaws, but he still regarded them with suspicion. Not surprising, considering where they were. No truly honest folk would stray so far into outlaw territory. However, he'd give them the benefit of the doubt.

'What are you doing out here, anyway?' Jim asked. 'Not that I'm complaining. We'd be dead meat by now if you hadn't rode in.'

'We've been sent in to apprehend Zachariah

Holmes,' the major unbent a little, 'since his gang have taken to attacking the railroad.' He paused, and there was some disdain in his voice when, after some moments, he went on. 'Some railway investors have powerful friends, Mr Murphy. Powerful enough to gain the ear of the President himself. The Holmes gang have finally gone too far. My column has orders to wipe them out unless they surrender themselves unconditionally.'

'Holmes is lying dead over there.' Jim pointed out the body. 'I take it we're free to go?' He still wasn't sure the major would allow them to leave.

'Is this your wagon?'

'Yes, Major.' Sera pasted her sweetest smile on her face and attempted to coax him into a better frame of mind.

'Then I'll have to give you a note in hand, sir. I'm obliged to tell you I have to commandeer it.' He didn't look in the least bit sorry, but Jim let that pass. 'We need a wagon like this to carry our supplies. You can cash the note in at the fort and buy yourself a better one on the proceeds.'

'You can't do that,' Sera exclaimed aghast. 'It's not for sale.'

The major was already scribbling into a notebook. 'It's done,' he told her curtly, 'and you're damned lucky I don't arrest you as well.'

'The wagon's ours – mine and Jim's.' Sera snuggled

close against Jim's side and gazed up at the army commander, ignoring his implicit threat. 'Fact is, Major,' she began to explain herself. 'Jim and I only got married recently and we're still on our honeymoon.'

Jim stared wide-eyed at her. She was a real actress, even down to the blush on her cheeks. Not that all the play-acting in the world would deflect the hard-eyed officer from his purpose.

'We were heading west to start a new life,' she continued.

'Wagon's facing east,' the major countered coldly.

'We were lost.' Jim put in his cent's worth, for all the good it would do them. 'This land all looks the same to me.'

'Then those horrible outlaws descended on us.' Sera managed to make it sound as if they'd been attacked for no good reason. Equally obviously, the major wasn't completely taken in by her version of events, but without any other testimony was forced to let his suspicions ride. 'So you see, we must keep that wagon.' She laid her head on Jim's chest and batted her eyes. 'For sentimental reasons, if nothing else.'

The major tore out the note and handed it to Jim with a peremptory nod. 'See the quartermaster. He'll cut you out a draught horse to carry your belongings. You can leave the animal at the fort too.' He politely tipped his hat towards Sera. 'I'm afraid you'll have to walk, ma'am, but I'll detail someone to load your chattels for you.'

'No need, Major,' Jim broke in. 'We haven't much, I'll pack it myself.'

'This isn't the way to the fort.' Sera had walked hand in hand with Jim ever since they'd left the cavalry detachment.

'No,' he agreed.

'We won't get paid for the wagon unless we go there.'

'When they discover the wagon has a false floor packed with hard liquor we won't get paid anyway. That hard-faced major will dispatch a runner to the fort to have us arrested. He was suspicious of our entering outlaw territory in the first place, and when he finds our cargo of whiskey he'll have good reason to suspect we were trading with the Holmes gang.'

'They were attacking us. Surely he could see they were our enemies?'

'A falling-out between thieves isn't unknown, or even uncommon,' Jim reminded her.

'We ought to follow them, get our wagon back,' persisted the girl. 'All that work for nothing!'

'Not quite,' Jim grinned. 'I packed those last two gold bars with our belongings. It's not the fortune we intended, but it'll provide us with a start in our married life.'

160